BLETHERING ON!

MICHAEL WALTERS

Trafford
PUBLISHING

Order this book online at www.trafford.com/08-0723
or email orders@trafford.com

Most Trafford titles are also available at major online book retailers.

Note for Librarians: A cataloguing record for this book is available from Library and Archives Canada at www.collectionscanada.ca/amicus/index-e.html

ISBN: 978-1-4251-8013-3

We at Trafford believe that it is the responsibility of us all, as both individuals and corporations, to make choices that are environmentally and socially sound. You, in turn, are supporting this responsible conduct each time you purchase a Trafford book, or make use of our publishing services. To find out how you are helping, please visit www.trafford.com/responsiblepublishing.html

Our mission is to efficiently provide the world's finest, most comprehensive book publishing service, enabling every author to experience success. To find out how to publish your book, your way, and have it available worldwide, visit us online at www.trafford.com/10510

www.trafford.com

North America & international
toll-free: 1 888 232 4444 (USA & Canada)
phone: 250 383 6864 • fax: 250 383 6804
email: info@trafford.com

The United Kingdom & Europe
phone: +44 (0)1865 722 113 • local rate: 0845 230 9601
facsimile: +44 (0)1865 722 868 • email: info.uk@trafford.com

10 9 8 7 6 5 4 3

DEDICATION.

This book is dedicated to my parents who have always been a constant source of support and encouragement.

CONTENTS

PREFACE

Starting a new career is a daunting time for anyone. However, it is something that many of us have faced, sometimes on several occasions. For a young man who had trained as a teacher, this should have been a time of some apprehension and excitement. It turned out to be a truly traumatic experience!

The book follows the initial year of teaching in a secondary school in the heart of the Durham coalfield during the mid 1970's; a time of pit closure and the destruction of Britain's coal mining industry.

It recounts some of the many humorous, tragic and often thought provoking situations encountered using anecdotes and stories involving the staff and children. It gives an insight into the impact of the pit closure on the people who lived there, particularly the children.

The book tells how unprepared the young teacher was, the help that he received and his route to survival. Above all, it is a personal view of 1970's secondary education in Britain, taking a light-hearted look at some of the everyday events that we have all experienced, such as: school dinners, sports day, school inspectors, snowballing and many more hopefully bringing back our own happy memories.

All of the characters in this book are fictitious, and any resemblance to actual persons, living or dead, is purely coincidental.

1

IN THE BEGINNING …

It was a Thursday morning early in March 1975 when that first small brown envelope came through the letter box. It must have been a Thursday because thirty odd years on it always seemed to be a Thursday when those brown envelopes arrived: those envelopes that make things change.

I was in my final year of teacher training at a well respected Yorkshire college but I had applied for a teaching post back in my home county of Durham. I was coming home at the end of the course to my family and the girl I love. Like most local authorities at the time Durham operated a "pool" for newly qualified teachers. You applied for a job anywhere in the authority and were interviewed by their representative, often an ex head teacher or inspector, rather than the head teacher of each individual school and if successful then you might be called for interview at a specific school – or so I thought.

As I opened that small brown envelope that all changed; in fact everything changed. I didn't realise then but at that moment my career as a teacher was about to begin and my life would never be quite the same again.

This wasn't a request for an interview it was a contract for a teaching post. If I signed I was in, with at least some sort of a job when my college course finally came to an end. I was amazed. I thought that my interview had been OK but this was a job offer at a time when teaching jobs were very scarce.

I had lived in Durham all my life; the only exception being those last few years in York, yet the job offer was for a school in a village which at first I thought I didn't know – Alton Grange. Then I remembered, years before in my primary school a student teacher had set up a pen pal scheme with children from a school in Alton Grange. At the time it seemed like miles away and I seem to remember that the exchange of letters only lasted for a few weeks. Other than that, I knew nothing of Alton Grange.

My parents were naturally pleased at the prospect of a job; it didn't really matter where - one of their sons a teacher! My mother began asking around among her friends for opinions of Alton Grange while I started the search of road maps and atlases (no internet to rely on). To my surprise I soon discovered that Alton Grange was another small Durham mining village just a few miles from my parent's home. The general consensus among my mother's friends was that it was a "canny" place, but a bit the worst for wear since the pit had closed. I was later to discover that the pit had indeed closed recently throwing much of the community out of work and in some cases out of their homes. However, the comment didn't really concern me too much since this was probably true of many other Durham villages, including the one that I had been brought up in, during that period of time. As the son of a Durham miner it sounded like a pretty reasonable proposition.

I spent that weekend wondering what the next step would be. My girlfriend and her friends who were also teacher training, couldn't believe that I'd been offered a job at a school without an interview by the head teacher! What to do – should I simply accept and return the signed contract or should I contact the school? Or perhaps I should turn it down and wait for other offers.

It seemed to me that the first thing to do was find the school and have a look at the catchment area. Perhaps this would help me make up my mind.

One of my mother's friends had relatives living in a village near to the school and a nephew that she thought might even attend it. She described the school as " like ours (the one in the village) with a playing field in front and the main buildings set up from it." She went on to say, "you can't miss it, as you come into the village the pit heap's on the left and the school's set up on the hill on the right."

Well there we were. Directions as clear as mud but keen to find out what this wonder village might be like. So off I went to reconnoitre this possible job hope; my future.

My little Wolsley Hornet, bought for the princely sum of £15 and "restored" to a road worthy condition by my brother, seemed to sense the anticipation in that journey as it struggled up one of the hills on the way. As I approached the village the directions began to make sense. Sure enough there was a large colliery waste tip, the pit heap, on the right of the approach road to the village but at the other side there was indeed a school enjoying an elevated position looking across the valley.

It was a typical Durham school built I suspect to a common pattern in the 1930's, and still in use in much of the county today. A single storey red brick building with large arch shaped windows and a slate roof. From that part of the road it looked quite impressive, in good repair and the immediate vicinity was a mixture of private and relatively modern council housing.

My first impressions were that it looked quite promising, particularly compared to one of my teaching practice school's in Middlesborough the year before. But it was the Easter holidays and there were few children about, in fact very few people at all. I drove around the area supposedly making objective judgements but looking back I think that the first sight of that little school on the hill and the idea that someone actually wanted me to work there, had already made my mind up for me.

I went back to college feeling very unsure until I talked to other students. Very few had any hope of an interview, yet alone a job offer. They all wondered what I was waiting for. In the end it seemed like too good an offer to turn down so I drafted a letter to the head teacher asking for an opportunity to visit the school while providing him with the chance to meet me and, if he wished, interview me, as I assumed that would be the normal practice. It took several attempts to write anything like an acceptable letter and even the final draft seemed totally inadequate. However, I posted it and tried to concentrate on the business of college – my final teaching practice in a grammar school in the middle of North Yorkshire.

About ten days later I went home for the weekend, the last one before starting that teaching practice, and another brown envelope greeted me. This time it was a very short letter, just three or four lines, from the headteacher offering me the opportunity to visit at any time and asking me to return the signed contract back to the local authority as soon as possible. There was no suggestion of an interview. I thought that this was a bit strange but being new to the process I contacted the school and spoke to the secretary who suggested that I should come into school as soon as possible but without specifying a time. I decided to go the following Wednesday morning.

Wednesday came all too quickly and I set off full of a mixture of enthusiasm, trepidation and a little confidence, dressed in my best suit; my only suit, a lovat green terylene with slight flares,trying to at least look the part. I headed for the building that I had seen on the hill those couple of weeks earlier. As I arrived I noticed that there didn't seem to be a car park, just a couple of rows of cars parked in part of the school yard. There were about ten, mostly four or five year old cars making my old banger look even more of a heap. Immediately I began feeling a bit inferior but as I looked for the entrance I was struck by the peeling paint on the window frames and the general poor state of repair to the building; the feeling of inferiority faded. I passed the side of a demountable classroom from which the clatter of typing could clearly be heard and opened a door into a long corridor. I was struck by the decoration and the smell: it was primary school all over again. It was that smell of stale school dinners: that smell that lingers and never fades, like stale cabbage, and it was certainly lingering!

It was about ten thirty. There was no one about and the silence was quite eerie. Just then a bell rang twice very loudly and the silence was shattered. Groups of scruffy looking teenagers in jeans and tatty leather jackets walked towards me, looking me up and down, the girls giggling, as they passed and went out of the door. They hardly seemed to notice me. They were followed by a big man in typical teacher dress – brown corduroy jacket and fawn trousers.

"Right lad, what can we do for you?" was his opening comment.

"I'm here for interview," I replied. "Oh," said the teacher, "interview, things are looking up. You'll need to see Arthur then. Come on, I'll take you down."

The teacher strode off. I followed like the little lamb that I felt.

" You're going to join us then, I'm another Arthur, Arthur Johnson hard sums and music," said the teacher and held out his hand. I shook hands and in a tongue tied reply blurted, "Michael Walters, science and maths." His eyebrows raised slightly and he seemed to mumble to himself, "another lamb to the slaughter."

We passed through what must have been an assembly hall and Arthur opened a door into what looked like a large cupboard. Inside was crammed with piles of papers, old registers, books and a large lady in her mid fifties sat with her back towards a roaring coal fire.

She put down the china cup that she was drinking from and looked me up and down.

" Jean, someone to see Arthur!" said the other Arthur. He turned to me "see you in September, I suppose," and off he went.

I smiled politely and tried to explain who I was and why I was there. The woman stood up without a word, turned to her right skilfully missing knocking over a mountain of papers and walked towards a door which looked like yet another cupboard. But she knocked on the door, opened it and walked into the room.

"There's a Mr. Walters to see you about the science job," said Jean, who turned out to be the school secretary.

" Nowt to do with me," came the reply, "he'll have to see Ned at the bottom school."

"Bottom school" and "Ned," what was he talking about? I must have come to the wrong school or got it wrong some other way. I'd come for an interview with the head teacher and something in a cupboard was telling me to go away, to go elsewhere.

Jean stepped back from the 'cupboard', I still had not seen its contents, and started to explain. It was a split site school formed some years before by the amalgamation of the former separate boys and girls schools. This had been the girls school and was now used as the upper school for older pupils and some specialist subjects like domestic science. 'Ned' was Mr. Edward Walker, currently the deputy head teacher who would be taking over as acting head teacher from Mr. Harris, the voice in the cupboard, in September.

She went on to explain that Ned usually worked from the lower school (bottom school), which was the former boys school in the front street.

I just stood and listened. All of this was news to me. I had no idea that another building existed, or that the school was split site. I began to feel even less confident, quite nervous in fact. I hadn't done my research very well and now felt vulnerable. I felt as if I hadn't done my homework properly and was about to be put in detention.

Jean moved back to her desk, sat down and picked up the telephone, which incidentally looked like something from a museum or a Will Hay film. "I'll just ring Ned and let him know you're on your way," she said. I couldn't help overhearing the call.

"Ned, there's a Mr. Walters here to see you," said Jean.

"Whe?" came the reply.

"Mr. Walters, about the science job in September," said Jean.

"Oh, bloody hell," balled the voice at the other end of the telephone line, "Can't Arthur see to him?"

I was beginning to think everyone in the school must be called Arthur as Jean said , "No Ned, Mr. Harris said that you should deal with it."

"Oh, bloody Hell," came the reply, "Right send him down and I'll see to him now, but it'll have to be quick: I'm teaching you know!"

"That'll be a first," Jean mumbled to herself.

Jean put the phone down and turned her attentions to me.

"Ned, that's Mr. Walker is the deputy head teacher at the moment but will be acting head teacher from September, he wants to see you at the bottom school, OK."

I said that it was fine and listened carefully to Jean's directions to the "bottom school."

A few minutes later I was back in the car trying to make sense of the directions. I set off but just couldn't find it. I drove up and down the Front Street but there didn't seem to be anything like a school. I thought about what Jean had said ,

"Its down passed the Co-op and into the Front street. It's a big old building on the left, you can't miss it."

Well, I had missed it. Then I thought about the words again. "An old building in the Front street." I'd driven past a very old almost derelict building a couple of times now. I wondered if that could be it. I was just about to park and find someone to ask when a boy in a scruffy brown bomber jacket came running out of the yard next to the building followed by a group of younger girls. This must be it I thought and my heart sank. Looking back I shouldn't have been surprised. It was a typical Durham mining village in the mid 1970's at a time when the colliery had just been closed – but hindsight is a wonderful thing!

The Front Street was a mixture of small shops, terraced houses and derelict boarded up buildings on the main road through the village. I drove up and down the street a few more times and slowly it began to dawn. The large semi-derelict building in the middle of the street, the one the children had come from: this was it.

The building had high rusty gates leading to a tarmac drive. As I drove in I could now see how this opened out into a tarmac yard. I parked the car in line with the other cars and my attention was drawn to a large circular stone in the gable end of the building. It had the date 1891 carved into the stone. Was this the date that the building had been built or just the last time that it had been painted! It reminded me of pictures I had seen of Victorian workhouses.

This must be the school. It was in a terrible state ; broken window boarded up with bits of ill fitting wood, a lawn growing in the guttering, drainpipes torn off leaving green damp walls and AGBB in large letters of red paint scrawled on any bit of wall. I wondered what I'd let myself in for.

I got out of the car and began looking for an entrance when a short, fat man smoking a pipe and wearing a blue boiler suit came out of a half door beneath the set of steps close to where I had parked. He turned out to be the caretaker and directed me to another set of steps at the other end of the building.

I pushed open the doors and was immediately hit by that stale school dinner smell again. I walked into the stone floored corridor, with a small cloakroom on the right with a staircase leading away from the corner. In front of me was yet another set of paint chipped blue doors. I could hear footsteps coming from beyond the doors but not the noise of children. I pushed my head through the double doors to be greeted by a stocky bespectacled man in a dark grey suit. He was smoking a cigarette and pacing backwards and forwards through the open doorway. He caught sight of me and cigarette still in mouth said,

" You must be Walters, I'll be with you in a minute."

He took the cigarette from his mouth and pushed his head into the classroom door where a class of children were working in silence. He balled at the children,

"Not a word from anyone while I'm busy talking to Mr. Watson, or I'll be back to give you all a dose of the stick!"

With that, he turned away, beckoned to me to follow and put the cigarette back in his mouth. I had met Ned!

We walked back through the double doors and across the cloakroom to a small winding staircase in the corner. It led to a doorway with the door marked "Headmaster." Ned pushed open the door to reveal yet another cupboard like room, larger than the previous one and with a small window near the ceiling in one wall and a large blazing coal fire in a black cast iron fireplace on the opposite wall. A cluttered desk was stood in front of the fire and Ned sat down with his back to the roaring fire. He looked at me, pointed at the chair in front of the desk and started to light another cigarette from the remains of the one in his mouth. I noticed the nicotine stained fingers commonly seen in the chain smoker.

Cigarette still in his mouth Ned said,

" Right lad, So you're going to start in September. You'll have sent the contract back to County, eh?"

I probably looked a little puzzled because this was not the sort of question that I was expecting. "Well, er, no, not yet," I stammered.

"Oh, Hell," said Ned, "Look lad we can't muck about, get the bugger sent back t'keep that lot right at County Hall!"

"So there's a job for me? You're quite happy with me. There aren't any questions you're like to ask me?" I asked.

"No, er no lad, there's nowt t'worry about, its all been sorted out," replied Ned.

Just at that moment there was a knock on the door and as it opened a tall man in a brown dust coat walked into the room, his glasses perched on his forehead. He was reading a piece of paper as he came through the door.

"Oh, sorry ,"said the man, "I didn't realise that you had someone in with you ,Ned."

Ned puffed away on his cigarette, not taking it from his mouth throughout the exchange, the cigarette bobbing up and down as he spoke.

"This is young Walton," Ned burbled, "he'll be a new starter in September."

"Walters," I said and moved to shake hands with the man who I assumed was the caretaker.

"Arthur Paterson," said the man as he shock hands "I'll be acting deputy to Ned from September." Another Arthur and another mistake: this man was the deputy head not the caretaker. I later discovered that he also taught woodwork, hence the dust coat.

With that Ned suddenly stood up and announced,

" Right then, that's all sorted and we'll see you in September and don't forget, send that bloody form back t'County!"

Ned moved towards the door but was stopped by Arthur.

"Er, perhaps, Mr. Walters, what's your first name lad? , has some questions?"

Before I could answer Ned broke in,

"Aye, wey you can deal with all that Arthur." Then in a total change of tone and voice Ned said a phrase I was to hear many times in the future.

"Are you staying for lunch?" This was Ned's posh voice.

"That would be nice," I heard myself saying automatically.

Arthur frowned and Ned burst out,

"Oh, bloody Hell I'll ha' to change the bloody dinner numbers."

"Well, if its any trouble," I began but Ned burst in,

"Grand, that's champion, perhaps when you come in September."

Ned bustled out of the room, lighting yet another cigarette. Then halfway down the stairs he called back,

"How, Arthur keep an eye on them buggers downstairs I'm away to the top school for me dinner."

Arthur's eyebrows raised. I was left standing in a half dazed state, obviously looking rather bemused by the whole episode, when Arthur began to speak,

"Well you're met Ned. He's a bit of a character but he'll be alright with you. Perhaps you'd like to meet some of the other staff and we can have a bit of a chat."

We left the room and went downstairs. As we started along the corridor we passed Ned's class. Arthur opened the door of the silent room. The children sprang to their feet.

"OK," said Arthur, "Mr. Walker's been called away, a smile went round the faces of the children, so just keep busy till the bell goes for dinner. Billy, I want you to come and tell me if anyone misbehaves."

Each classroom seemed full of poorly dressed scruffy children, many looking quite small for their age but all working busily in silence. There was no sign of a uniform, but equally no sign of chaos or disruption. At the front of each class was a succession of "typical" teachers. I was introduced to a selection of them then went into the woodwork room with Arthur, where he had a class working on a variety of jobs. Just glancing around the room was a real insight. There was a total mixture of boys from the timid to the gang like thug but all seemed completely at ease with their particular task, obviously knowing what to do and how to do it.

Arthur gave me a brief review of the school's curriculum structure and told me that everything was in a bit of a turmoil with the sudden and unexpected retirement of the present head teacher but he assured me that it was a good school and that he hoped everything would be ready when I started teaching in September.

Arthur was a sincere man and looking back I'm sure that he meant his reassurances and I believed him, besides as everyone kept telling me, "it was a start and jobs were hard to find."

So I took the job and sent back the contract to County Hall just as Ned had insisted. The real changes were about to begin.

2

NEW STARTERS...

With Ned's comments still ringing in my ears, I went back to College at the end of the Easter break. Alton Grange and the new job had to take second place for a few weeks while I concentrated on my final teaching practice. But now it all seemed different: a sense of purpose and a goal to achieve. It was real.

It was hard not to make comparisons, even then, between Alton Grange and my final placement in a rural grammar school in North Yorkshire. But I had no idea of how different things would really be in September.

The weeks passed quickly. Teaching practice was hard work and time consuming but all the time I knew that a real job would be there in September, something many of my friends were still worried about.

The summer seemed to pass quickly. I was working as a relief postman with very early starts and a split shift day. I was always grateful for the work but the hours were pretty awful. Then the next thing that I knew it was the first Monday in September and I'd heard absolutely nothing from school; no welcome pack, no directions, no class lists, nothing and no sign of a timetable. I was very apprehensive and although everyone tried to be supportive this was going to be one of those things that you just have to face and get on with.

I thought that I'd better try to look the part, try to hide my inexperience, not realising that everyone, especially the children, would be able to see straight through it. So off I went dressed in a brown tweed jacket and brown trousers with a plain cream shirt and brown tie. Very much the "typical" teacher I thought and modelled on the men that I'd seen on the visit. It had cost me a large part of my summer job pay but hopefully it would be worth it.

I arrived at school at half past eight trying to be reasonably early without appearing too keen. I assumed that I could be working in the Lower School premises and was rather surprised to see no other cars parked in the yard as they had been the previous Easter. Anyway, I was there after a journey that had seemed like two days across the desert but in fact was about twenty minutes, ready to start teaching.

I walked into the staffroom and came face to face with a short, stout elderly man in a blue boiler suit. I didn't recognise him as the man I'd seen in the yard the previous Easter. He was carrying a bucket of dirty water and clouds of foul smelling smoke billowed from a grubby pipe set in the corner of his mouth. "What do yer want?" he grunted.

"I'm one of the staff, a new teacher," I replied.

"Oh, a new starter, I thought you were here too early, a bit keen, eh? t'others'll not be here till about ten two. I've put the fire on, it'll take the damp off that wall a bit, boilers still leaking in Paterson's room."

He pushed past me and disappeared down the corridor, smoke still pouring from his pipe like a steam train hauling a heavy load as it moved out of the station. So much for not being too keen!

I looked around at the staffroom. It reminded me of an old railway station waiting room with its black cast iron fireplace with cracked and broken tiles in the hearth, a dirty brown oil cloth floor covering and a collection of odd chairs. The frequent belches of smoke coming back down the chimney completed the picture. At the far end of the room a window had obviously been removed and a flat roofed extension had been built extending the room forming something of an annex. The ceiling was covered in brown marks showing all the signs of rain damage. It housed a much battered dining table and chairs. The floor was littered with piles of cardboard boxes, most filled with what looked like rubbish.

I was also struck by the smell, a smell I'd smelt many times before. I looked a little more closely at one of the boxes and there was the answer – Banda fluid, the liquid used to duplicate worksheets and the like at that time. I had clearly remembered the smell from my own schooldays. The highly flammable liquid was leaking from one of the cans inside the box only feet away from the roaring open coal fire.

As I stood taking in the scene a face appeared at the window in the top part of the door. "Alright then," said the young man in a friendly confident manner, as he walked through the door. "You new then?"

"Michael Walters, science, just starting this morning," I spluttered.

"Jeff Gray, general dogs body but that'll be your job now, survived since last Easter. Don't look so worried, you'll be OK here. Have you met Ned yet, what a nutter!"

Already I was beginning to feel a bit more reassured yet still apprehensive about the job.

Jeff explained that he was sharing lifts with Arthur Johnson, the man that I had met the previous Easter, and had been dropped off early. No one ever came early and he usually put the kettle on to make some tea. I soon learned the importance of tea to teachers. The kettle boiled and Jeff poured the tea into what looked like another kettle, but was in fact a heavy green metal tea pot which he put on the hearth close to the fire. He began telling me what a canny place it was and that were lots of good people working there but he made no mention of the children.

Just then the door burst open and a tall middle aged woman walked in.

"Tea made Jeff," she said as she picked up the tea pot from the hearth.

"He's a good lad," she said as she felt the weight of the tea pot, then noticing me she said, "Oh, hello, you'll be one of the new starters then?"

"Yes," I replied, but before I could say anything else the door opened and several people walked into the room which was now becoming a bit crowded. The group of people started talking among themselves seemingly oblivious of my presence. I looked at the clock on the wall in the alcove opening – it was ten to nine. They all sat down having poured themselves cups of tea.

I sat waiting for something to happen as the clocked ticked past nine o'clock but they all just continued to chat amongst themselves about holidays, football and politics with no mention of school. About ten past nine, the man that I had now recognised as the deputy head that I'd met at Easter, seemed to notice my attention being drawn to the clock and looked at his watch.

" I suppose we'll have to make a start," he said, "there's been some bother with the timetable but young Michael here – he pointed towards me- will sort most of that out."

I wondered what he meant and felt most uncomfortable – what was this trouble and how was I going to sort it out? The tall woman turned to Arthur but looked at me.

"Another lamb to the slaughter," she said. Arthur made no reply.

Arthur gave out hand written copies of a temporary timetable to the staff, who almost immediately started moaning about them, then someone stood up and said, "What the Hell's this, CA?"

Arthur looked at the piece of paper,

"Ah, right, this was one of Ned's ideas – Current Affairs- it's a way of keeping the kids informed about things in the news."

"Ned's ideas," said the man, "Ned never had an idea in his life, it's a gash lesson isn't it, a fill in 'cos you can't make the timetable fit ?"

"Well, er, yes," said Arthur, "I told you, we've had a bit of trouble with the timetable."

Another lady sprang to Arthur's defence,

"Don't be so miserable, Peter. At least we've got a timetable this year."

"Yes we have," said Arthur defensively, "but bear in mind it's only temporary at the moment, there's still some problems on staffing to sort out and things might change."

"Here we go again," said Peter Milburn.

I was taking all of these comments in with some amazement – at least we've got a timetable; how could you work without one? As I looked at my timetable I began to wonder just what sort of school I had come to work in.

Just then Peter began to speak again,

"Last year it was after tatie picking week before we had a timetable, d'yer remember Ned; Whe's had nee maths?"

I had expected to teach science to a range of classes with perhaps some specialist biology teaching in the upper school, after all that's what I'd been trained to do. Science did appear on my timetable: one class, 2C for two double lessons a week, the rest was Maths and English with some of the "new" Current Affairs lessons thrown in for good measure.

Arthur looked at me, my face must have been giving away my feelings as he said,

"Not quite what you expected, they fill you with all that crap at college about teaching only one specialism, but this is the real world. Some people are still teaching everything to one class like they do in primary schools. We thought you'd be better off finding your feet here in the bottom school. It'll give you time to get used to the kids in this God forsaken hole."

I was so taken aback, feeling vulnerable and unsure of myself that I didn't argue. I said nothing, although my head was full of questions; what did I know about teaching English? Could I cope with the lessons? Was there a scheme of work? Who would help me? Why was about a third of my whole timetable with one class, 2B? Did I have a registration group? Lots of other questions were zipping through my mind, but who could I ask? I didn't know anyone.

By now it was about twenty past nine and we were still sat in the staffroom. We could hear children shouting in the yard and see boys hanging about the entrance to the outside toilets at the bottom of the yard, as plumes of smoke issued from the building. No one seemed concerned about the time. Suddenly the door burst open and Ned stormed in,

"Time y'er got them in, Arthur," snorted Ned, "then I can get these damned dinner registers sorted out."

"I thought you'd be busy at the top school," replied Arthur.

"Can't work up there, with that bloody woman next door. I've told Jack to light the fire in the office down here each day and I'll work from there," replied Ned. Arthur's face dropped and he said nothing for a few minutes.

"Well folks, best make a start. Let's line them up and sort them out," said Arthur.

I was quickly to learn that Ned had been the bane of Arthur's life for many years and his appointment as Acting Headteacher had come as a great relief to Arthur who had expected Ned to work with the secretary in the office at the Upper School buildings. The reference to school dinners was also to take on huge significance.

One of the staff picked up a hand bell and set off down the corridor to a set of double doors near the cloakroom and a staircase which led to the office that Ned had talked about. There were to be no automatic bells here: it reminded me of my primary school. We all followed down the corridor to a set of steep stone steps that led into the school yard. The teacher rang the bell loudly and immediately children ran towards the steps forming parallel lines down the yard facing the steps to the entrance. The children who were just beginning their secondary schooling milled about bemused by all that was going on. Arthur appeared at the top of the steps and looked at the children. Those who were in lines stopped talking and stood silently looking at Arthur.

Arthur shouted,

"New starters, line up over here."

He pointed to the left of the lines of children. I felt like joining the line of new starters. There was something in the tone of Arthur's voice that made you realise immediately that he was in charge and wasn't to be messed about. I stood and watched in amazement as what had been an unruly rabble of unkempt young hooligans were now standing as meekly as lambs. Nothing had been said or done, it just happened. Arthur turned to the staff,

" We'll have the second and third years in, then I'll go through the first year class lists. If Mr Walters and Mr Chapman could stay here with me, everyone else collect their classes as they come in."

The staff all seemed to know what was happening, as did the children. Peter Milburn, the metalwork teacher who had moaned about the Current Affairs lessons, beckoned to the line at the far left. Immediately a stream of children started coming up the steps in single file and into the building. It was all very orderly and totally silent, quite military really – and not by accident I was to discover later.

As the penultimate boy of the first line approached the steps he suddenly fell to the ground. I assumed that he had tripped, then he began thrashing about uncontrollably: he was obviously having a fit of some sort, perhaps an epileptic fit. I wondered what would happen but before anyone could attempt to help the boy Ned appeared in the doorway. He had just come down the corridor and had missed the previous events. He was finishing a cigarette, which was perched in the corner of his mouth.

"Come on, hurry up, get them in I've these bloody registers to do," he snorted, the cigarette moving rapidly up and down but not falling from his mouth.

"Eh, Mr Walker," said Brian Chapman, "One of them's fainted or something." "Oh, bloody Hell," yelled Ned, "And I've got these registers to sort out. "Jeff," he turned to Jeff Gray who was still waiting to bring in his class as the children had been stopped from coming in while the fitting child was dealt with, "Fetch a fire blanket from the science room."

Jeff ran off and quickly returned with a tatty grey blanket with a large hole burned through one end.

"Hoy it over the little bugger then," yelled Ned.

The blanket was thrown over the child thrashing about on the ground while the other children looked on in amazement.

"Right, they can just step over him as they come in. Mind you don't stand on him," yelled Ned at the children as they negotiated the wildly moving arms and legs. There was no panic or commotion and no one questioned what had happened, or the action that Ned had instigated. I was gob smacked; I couldn't believe what I'd seen. The other "new starters" looked equally dazed.

By the time that the last class had gone into the building the thrashing blanket had stopped moving and a bewildered boy started crawling out from it. He stood up, without help, looking around for the other children.

"Come on, lad, sort yourself out," called Arthur, "and take that blanket back to Mr Gray. Hurry up, shift yourself!"

The young boy brushed himself off and ran up the steps towards the entrance.

"Blanket, blanket," yelled Arthur.

The boy came back picked up the blanket and ran back into school. The "new starters" were still standing in the yard, now in complete silence probable wondering what was going to happen next.

"Now let's get this lot sorted," said Arthur turning to Brian Chapman and myself, "there's only two classes coming in so you can have 1A Michael and Brian can have 1B. I'll read the names out and we can line them up properly."

Arthur turned back to the bewildered youngsters and spoke slowly and calmly to them but there was an authority in the tone of his voice which gave a very clear message – listen carefully and do exactly as you are told. The children moved into two lines with one exception. One boy was left not knowing where to go or what to do. Arthur looked at the boy,

"Stoddart, what's your problem?" he asked.

I was most impressed: how could he know the child's name when he'd only just started the school.

"Please sir, I'm Ian Jones ," started the boy."

"Jones?" said Arthur, "you're not on my list. There's no Jones here."

There was a pause as Arthur checked the lists of names.

"Sure you're not Stoddart?" said Arthur.

The boy shook his head.

"Well you look like the other Stoddart's we've had, (probably got the same father, he said to us) so we'll just call you that for now and that'll keep my paperwork right, OK."

The boy didn't know what to do and joined the remainder of 1B as Stoddart. I didn't know at the time but Ian Jones was to remain as Stoddart in Arthur's eyes for the rest of the time that he was in school.

These two incidents were typical of those early days in school. The blind obedience of the children and the total control of the teachers, which are now a thing of the past; whether that is such a bad thing is a debatable point. I was left realising that college had done little to prepare me for the real nitty gritty day to day experiences of teaching. I was rapidly realising that the real learning was about to begin and to say that it would be a baptism of fire would be an under statement.

Arthur handed me a copy of the timetable for 1A and a temporary register. "Just get them to copy down the timetable and begin sorting out the register," he said, "Ned' ll be along shortly to see about dinner money."

I shepherded the children into the first classroom. There was a real mixture ranging from long haired boys to an almost shaven headed girl with BEN tattooed on her left hand in large red letters. As there was no school uniform the children were dressed in a wide variety of clothing, many of them decidedly dirty. But they were all bright eyed and polite as they filed through the door into that dismal room. I'd just introduced myself and started filling in the register with their names when Ned came bounding in, the door almost torn from its hinges. There was no knock on the door or apology for the interruption, or indeed any explanation of who he was or what he was going to do, just that booming voice.

"What class is this?" he yelled.

"1A, Mr. Walker," I replied.

"Can't be, can't be!" yelled Ned as he shuffled some white meals registers. Then looking at the girl directly in front of him he said,

"What's your name pet?."

His tone of voice was completely different from before.

"Jacqueline Atkinson," replied the girl confidently.

"Oh, bloody Hell, not another Atkinson," snarled Ned as he looked at the registers. He went on, " There's nee Atkinson on this register. You're in the wrong bloody class, girl!"

With that he picked up the registers and stormed off out of the room. The children and I were equally surprised by this behaviour and did not realise that it was quite normal for Ned. Jacqueline stood up and started walking towards the door.

"My brother says Mr. Walker's balmy," said Jacqueline.

"That's enough of that, just sit down for the moment," I said "Mr Walker's obviously very busy and comments like that aren't necessary and won't be tolerated."

The girl's head dropped and she looked suitably subdued. She sat down. Little was I to know how often I would find myself defending Ned's actions or explaining what had happened.

Just then Arthur appeared at the door,

"Sorry to interrupt," he said, "but could you send any children with dinner money to the staffroom when its convenient."

"But Mr. Walker's just been in and," I started.

"Yes, I know," replied Arthur, "we've sorted it out. Just send the dinner money people to the staffroom."

I looked at the class,

"Right then, anyone who stays for school dinners needs to go to the staffroom just across the corridor. A little boy towards the back of the class raised his hand.

"What's the problem?" I asked.

"Please sir, I used to get free dinners at the last school so do I get them here?" he said.

"Er, I suppose so," I answered not at all sure of my reply, "perhaps you'd better go to the staffroom as well and ask Mr. Walker. Does anybody else have free meals?"

About two thirds of the class put their hands up.

" OK, you'll all need to go to the staffroom," I said thinking that if there was a register of school meals they would need to be recorded on it. The children stood up and began leaving the room. I expected some to remain but they all left their seats. I thought that I'd better go with them.

We crossed the corridor and lined up on the left hand side outside the staffroom. The top part of the staffroom door was glass and as I looked through I could see Ned sitting at the table at the back of the room reading a newspaper. I knocked on the door.

"Come in," called Ned in a gruff harsh voice.

"Its 1A school dinner money, Mr. Walker," I said.

"Send them in, then," snapped Ned.

"But its all of 1A, Mr. Walker," I replied, "some of them think they'll be on free meals."

"Oh, bloody Hell," snarled Ned , "I suppose I'll ha' to sort it out."

Ned got up from his seat, seemed to sprint across the staffroom and pushed past me out into the corridor.

"Oh, bloody Hell," he snarled as he saw the long line of children.

He started shouting at the children.

"Right, those paying for their dinners, stand over there."

He pointed to the right hand side of the corridor. Two children moved across the corridor. Ned continued to snarl at the children,

"Those of you that got free dinners at your primary school stay where you are and those who's fathers are too bloody idle to work, stand in the middle."

Most of the children stayed at the left hand side of the corridor, three moved to the middle and two small girls started to cry, clearly not knowing what to do and frightened by this snarling mad man in front of them.

"And you can switch the water works off," snapped Ned, "its simple enough make you're mind up!"

With that Ned turned, went back into the staffroom and shut the door. We all stood speechless in the corridor dazed by what we'd just been through. It was the first day in a new school for these children, everything was traumatic anyway and here was this lunatic yelling insults at everyone. The two little girls that were crying just didn't know what to do and expected some understanding not to be shouted at. I was trying to console them and sort out the problem when Arthur appeared at the end of the corridor. His woodwork room was just around the corner and he had probably heard the commotion in the corridor.

"Hey come on, no tears this is a new start today, a new school, we should all be pleased ," he said to the two girls, "now lets sort this out."

He moved the girls away from the other children and talked to them further down the corridor, while I knocked on the staffroom door again opened it and walked in with the first of the children who was paying for there school meals.

I turned and walked out back into the corridor before anything could be said.

Wc could hcar Ncd talking to thc child, who quickly rcappcarcd in the corridor and said "Next." Arthur returned the two girls to the group putting them both in the middle line. He looked at me with a look that says everything that needs to be said without speaking. Then he said,

"You'll be OK now, just keep sending them in, Ned' ll sort it out. The primary school didn't send any details on who was on free meals and so on, so it'll need to be sorted out." He smiled, glanced in through the staffroom door where Ned was sat like Ebennezer Scrouge counting the dinner money and recording it in the register, then walked back up the corridor looking in to the classrooms as he passed.

The rest of the day passed with little incident. I floundered around finding things for the children to do as I discovered ancient textbooks in the cupboard. There was no scheme of work, no worksheets or appropriate induction materials. It all came from the teacher: straight off the top of my head! I was quickly learning what real teaching was all about and it was all new to me. The mysteries of the daily routine gradually became clearer as those first few days passed. Just as 1A were "new starters," it must have been obvious that I was also in the same position. However, I was not alone; two other new members of staff were also beginning their teaching careers – Rick Morson, a very young looking history and geography teacher and Sarah Browne, a lady in her forties who had qualified as a mature student and expected to teach art. Both had been given registration classes in the upper school so I was not to meet them until later in the week.

When we did meet and exchange our thoughts about those first few days the general consensus was that Alton Grange was a pretty unusual place, nothing like any of our previous experiences on teaching practice or our own school lives, but it was full of caring people with the interests of the children at heart – even Ned in his own peculiar way!

3

LEARNING TO COPE.

Those first few weeks were the steepest learning curve that I'd ever had to face, far more difficult than teaching practice or anything at college. I had taken the post at Alton Grange expecting to teach science. The "temporary timetable" lasted a few days before it had to be abandoned because one of the long term sick staff died suddenly and there was obviously going to be a delay before a new appointment could be made. Supply staff were difficult to find at that time, school's relying largely on teachers who had recently retired or just moved into the area. I found myself without a proper timetable teaching anything "off the top of my head" most of the time on a day to day basis. Little did I know but this was likely to go on for several weeks. I'm sure the more experienced staff didn't like it but found it easier to cope because they had built up a bank of stand alone lessons to draw on in such situations. As a new teacher this wasn't going to happen and every lesson was a new lesson. However, it was amazing how quickly everything began to fall into a routine and on the face of it the children were being taught in a meaningful way. I'm sure that today's educational experts would have been appalled but the standards of teaching, learning and behaviour were much better than my most recent experience. That said Ned's daily morning trauma, until a proper timetable was established, was an experience in itself.

"Arthur, whe's had nee maths?" snorted Ned, just as Peter Milburn had predicted.

This was a typical start to Monday mornings in those initial weeks of teaching. At first I just couldn't believe it but I quickly learned that the secret of success was the ability to adapt to the situation.

"Er, 2B didn't seem to have much last week, Ned," replied the calm controlled voice of Arthur, the deputy head, who was checking a list on a clipboard.

"Right then," said Ned scanning the teachers sat in the staffroom drinking tea as they waited for Ned's decree and desperately trying to avoid eye contact. "Walters, you can take 2B for Maths this morning and English this s'afternoon." "Certainly Mr. Walker," I began to reply but a deathly hush had filled the room. "Do you really think so, Ned?" asked Arthur, an air of concern in his voice. "Oh, aye," said Ned, "the lad's got to learn how to cope."

With that Ned turned and looked directly at me.

"Look, lad you'll be OK, just remember don't hit anyone after three o'clock, but if you do have to, hit them as hard as you can!"

I looked back in complete disbelief at these words of wisdom not quite knowing what they meant or what to expect. I can't remember what else was said in that morning timetabling sort out as a feeling of dread and trepidation had already set in. In what seemed like seconds but must have been about ten minutes the rest of the lower school staff were allocated their classes for the day.

This was a split site school with children in years 1-3 housed in the older dilapidated buildings in the Front Street – the children called it the bottom school – and years 4 and 5 in a slightly more modern traditional1930's style building –the top school.

At my original "interview" I had found the top school, assuming it to be the whole school but had been redirected by the secretary to the bottom school to meet Ned. I then turned up at the bottom school on the first school day in September not knowing whether I would be working there or at the other building. It seemed that just by chance I would spend my first year teaching children in years 1-3. I was told that this was not the case some weeks later.

I walked out of the staffroom and down the corridor to what would become my classroom. It had been used by Ned when he was a classroom teacher some years before but had not been in use for some time as was very evident as I opened the door noticing the worn wooden threshold that prevented the door from closing properly. There were no pictures or posters on the walls just a tide mark at about six feet from the floor – I found out much later in my teaching career that this was the height that the cleaners were allowed to work to within their Health and Safety rules. The windows on the outside wall faced onto the Front Street but were too high to see through and their lower panes had been fitted with heavily patterned glass or were boarded up. The desks looked as if they had been delivered directly from a museum and an air of "Dotheboys Hall" filled the room. But before I could take it all in the children started to arrive. They had been told to line up outside the room and wait quietly until their teacher was ready to greet them. To my amazement that's exactly what they did.

"Right, come on in then," I called, "take a seat."

The children filed past me into the room, each looking me up and down in their own way and no doubt making a judgement. I tried hard to look as I thought an experienced teacher would, someone who knew exactly what he was doing, but it must have been obvious that I was new to the job. I had made a real effort and was wearing my best green suit, my only suit at the time, and a pair of green platform boots (fashionable at the time) to be a bit more trendy, thinking that it might help me to be accepted by the children.

The children sat down in silence. I tried to close the door but it wouldn't shut.

"Doesn't close, sir," said a girl sitting nearby. "Mr Walker didn't close it 'cos he always walked in and out smoking his tabs when he was in here sometimes last year."

I looked puzzled at the girl and initially said nothing thinking I'd find out later from the staff what it all meant.

"Thank you," I replied, "OK, let's take the register. I want you to answer your names as I call them out."

This seemed like a straightforward start until I looked at the hand written pencil list in front of me. It was a temporary register just in case anyone needed to move classes.

"You'll have to bear with me if I get your name wrong. I've only got surnames and initials on this list and they're going to be difficult to read," I said to the class.

"But you're the teacher," called out a long haired boy from the back of the room, "don't you know what you're doing?"

"And you are?" I asked sternly.

"Can't remember," said the boy, "none of us can remember, can we?"

His eyes scanned the class and many of the children's heads dropped or tried to avoid eye contact. Panic must have been written across my face as I thought that trouble was about to begin and I hadn't even taken the register. Just at that moment the half closed door opened and Arthur walked in, a scruffy looking boy following him.

"Sorry to interrupt, but this one's yours, a Stephenson I think," said Arthur looking at the boy then beckoning to me to hand over the register. "Ah, yes," said Arthur seeing the list, "one of Ned's scrawl, I'll do this if you like, it's a bit of a mess."

Arthur pushed his glasses up onto his forehead and holding the list close to his face started to call the surnames. The children all answered immediately and very politely. Throughout Arthur's visit there wasn't a word out of place. I was learning an enormous amount in those few minutes just by watching the response of the children to this very experienced practitioner. The long haired boy turned out to be Joe Dawson; strange how he couldn't remember his name when I'd asked but remembered it immediately when it was called out by Arthur.

"Thanks," said Arthur moving his glasses back into position, " I'll be back in a while. I'm keeping an eye on this lot today."

Arthur left the room and I looked directly at Dawson for what seemed like hours but could only have been seconds until he turned away from my stare. I didn't say anything. I had realised on teaching practice that it was often not what was said that mattered but the eye contact and what was not said providing no opportunity for a verbal response or confrontation. I didn't realise it at the time but those few words from Arthur and my response to Dawson were to give me a tolerable day, which would otherwise have turned into a nightmare.

"OK 2B it's Maths this morning, fractions," I said trying to be lively, positive and interesting. "Who can tell me what we mean by a fraction of something?" I asked the class. There was no response.

"Come on, what's a fraction?" I tried again.

"Don't you know, sir?" said a girl to my left.

"Yes, but I'm trying to get you to think about it," I replied.

"Thinking about it's alright," said the girl, " but we don't know the answers." She also scanned the class with that look that I now recognise says "don't you dare say a word." Fortunately the earlier experiences of the day and the few tricks that I'd picked up on teaching practice had prepared me for some of the scams that children play on new teachers and I wasn't about to let this cause a problem.

"Right, well we'd better find another way. Turn to page 73 of this book, when you get one," I said as I held up the textbook.

I asked the two boys sitting nearest to the door to give out a pile of old dog- eared Maths textbooks.

"We did these last year," shouted a girl from the back of the class.

"Oh good," I replied, "you'll be able to do the first one for us on the blackboard then."

"Can't remember," said the girl.

"Look's like no one can remember very much, perhaps we all need to read page 73 then write down the worked examples while we think about it and try to remember how to add these fractions," I said looking at the whole class and using the same scanning technique that both Dawson and the girl at the back of the room had used.

"Can't read or write," said another small boy who was sat very close to a radiator at the corridor side of the room.

"I'm sure that's not true. Come on, make an effort lad, let's see what you can do. You might surprise yourself especially since Mr. Johnson was just telling me the other day how good 2B was at Maths,"I replied my tone beginning to change as I could see what was starting to happen.

It was the usual game that many of these children tried on most of their teachers, determined to avoid learning or work of any description. Unfortunately for 2B they did not know at that stage just how determined I could be, and I was not having any of this "can't remember" routine.

Most children began to read the passage in the book then start to copy down the examples. One or two comments could be heard in the quiet chatter that went on as the children started to work,

"I remember doing these with Mr. Walker: you find a number that they all divide into and….."

Relief came in the form of the break time bell. We had started late, had the register fiasco and failed to do the introduction to fractions but at least I'd made it to the end of the lesson without too much trouble.

"Everyone finished the first five examples," I was saying as the door opened and in walked Arthur.

"Everything OK?" he asked.

"Fine, thank you," I replied, " but because we were a bit late starting I'm just making sure that everyone's done the first five examples."

"Splendid," said Arthur looking around the class. "How many have you done, Dawson?" asked Arthur looking directly at the boy.

"Two, sir" replied Dawson.

"Well you'd better get cracking then, or you'll end up without a break. Mr. Walters and I have one or two things to talk about while you're busy," replied Arthur.

Dawson's face was a picture. He was annoyed but didn't dare show it.

Arthur waited and chatted to me while the last few children completed their five fractions, including Dawson who had miraculously suddenly remembered how to do them.

" I thought I'd start the lesson tomorrow with a cake cut into fractions," I said to Arthur.

"Good idea," he said, "as long as you keep a piece for me."

As the last few children left the room the conversation was about me: the new teacher. Arthur and I were heading down the corridor for what was left of break as the children went in the opposite direction towards the exit to the playground. Dawson could be clearly heard in a deliberately raised voice, "What a berk, we'll have him after break."

" I liked him," said a tall girl, "you should let him alone."

Dawson turned on the girl snarling,

" I say what goes on in there. He's a teacher, so he's had it, right!"

"Oh OK, keep your hair on," said the girl backing down but clearly not impressed.

" You two, out, get some fresh air," shouted Arthur.

I didn't know whether he'd heard the comments but I knew that trouble was brewing for next lesson. Then Arthur said,

" He's a nasty piece of work, Dawson, but you'll get the better of him. That was a good move keeping him back to complete his work. He didn't like it but it was the first move towards respect. He needs to know who's in charge, then he can actually do some reasonably good work. Don't expect it all to come together at once. Just keep plugging away and be firm and consistent."

This was one of the first pieces of excellent advice that I received from Arthur. I didn't know it at the time but he was to be a superb support throughout the year. He didn't tell you exactly what to do, just gave sound advice and strategies to try. I never forgot those invaluable chats and used the technique myself many years later as head of department.

We must have been the last people to arrive at the staffroom which was full of staff all huddled around the open fire holding cups of tea.

"There's tea in the pot, Mike. Pour Arthur and yourself a cup," said Margaret pointing at a large green kettle like container on the hearth.

" How did you get on with 2B? There's some right one's in that lot," she continued.

" Oh, they were alright," I replied wondering whether Arthur would say anything, but he didn't comment.

"A bit awkward, I suppose, but that's only to be expected with a new teacher," I continued.

" Don't think like that, lad," said Peter, sitting in an armchair by the fire, "they'll have you, if you give them an inch. Give them a hard time, all the time until they know whose in charge."

Arthur interrupted Peter who seemed to be getting on his soap-box,

" What are you doing next?" he asked.

I wasn't sure how to answer: was he trying to find out if I knew what I was doing? Did he want to offer some help? Was there some other motive?

" Er, I thought that we might write an essay about their holidays," I replied quietly.

" I think I'd leave that for now if I was you and give them something to keep them busy while you watch them and weigh them up. Brian, you'll not be needing those First Aid in English books next lesson, send them in for Mike. You'll find loads of straightforward things in there for them to do while you get on top of the situation. Just a suggestion," said Arthur.

"Right, Arthur" said Brian not taking much notice, " where's young Harrison gone, break's going to be over before he's back with me tabs."

" You've been told about that," said Arthur " you're not to send kids out for cigarettes."

" But he's only gone next door to Albert's," said Brian.

Just then there was a knock at the door and a scruffy looking urchin opened the door.

" Got yer tabs, Mr Chapman," said the scruffy child.

Brian got to his feet and began moving towards the boy, who was already backing away. Arthur sprang to his feet moving into the gap between Brian and the boy.

"Well done ,son," said Arthur, "off you go now, keep the change."

The little boys face change from anxiety to a broad smile as he scurried away.

"That was a fiver," said Brian.

" I told you not to send kids for cigarettes just last week," said Arthur forcefully, " it's a hard life, if you make it one."

Brian sat down clearly annoyed but said nothing. The rest of the staff continued chatting ignoring the situation.

"It's about time we had them in," said Arthur opening the staff-room door. "Stoddart, go and ring the bell," he said to a boy walking down the corridor. The boy took no notice. Arthur called after him,

"Stoddart did you hear me?"

The boy stopped and turned around.

"Did you mean me,sir ?" he asked.

"Yes you," replied Arthur.

"But I'm not Stoddart ," said the boy. "I'm Ian ….."

"Ok, OK we've had this before, haven't we," said Arthur remembering an incident when the boy had started the school "my mistake, but you look very like Stoddart. Anyway, go and ring the bell and in future don't be in the wrong place at the wrong time."

The boy looked puzzled but ran off down the corridor to ring the bell.

Break over it was back to 2B English for me and I thought I'd better take the deputy head's advice as I wanted to show willing and it would be wise to bow to experience. The children came back into class louder than before with far more chair shuffling, chatter and general noise. I looked at the two girls sat directly in front of me,

"Pop along to Mr. Chapman's room and ask for the First Aid in English books, please," I said.

The girls looked at each other, started to laugh then left their seats and disappeared out of the door. A few minutes later they returned minus the books.

"He says he hasn't got them, just a first aid kit," said one of the girls.

That's great I thought, he's taking the staffroom incident out on me.

"Right, OK, thanks girls," I replied. I spent the next few minutes settling the class down then thought I'd better go back to my original idea: the holidays story.

" What did you do in the holidays?" I asked the class.

"Nowt," shouted out Dawson, "and neither did anyone else."

The majority of the class started to laugh and whistle loudly.

I was beginning to feel a sense of panic. A new inexperienced teacher faced with a class of very challenging children and no resources or materials ready to use. I was learning the most important lesson of teaching the hard way: always be prepared, have a contingency up your sleeve and don't show any lack of confidence or fear. Just then there was a knock at the door and Arthur walked in. Thank God I thought. I knew that this couldn't keep happening but for that immediate few seconds it seemed like a Godsend. The class stopped laughing and whistling instantly.

" Sorry to interrupt," said Arthur, "I had a feeling Brian wasn't really listening so I thought I'd drop these in, just in case they would be useful.

"Thanks very much," I said, "I'd intended to use them."

"Right, good, well in that case perhaps you two could give these books out," said Arthur to the two girls that I had previously asked.

The girls now did exactly as they were told with no laughter or silliness just following the instruction that they had been given.

"Turn to page 11, everybody," went on Arthur, "read the passage, then answer the questions in complete sentences. What's a complete sentence, Dawson?" asked Arthur.

"One where they don't let you out early," replied Dawson a smile on his face. Arthur looked directly at Dawson,

" I asked you because I was sure that you could give the correct answer not some silly response. It isn't clever. Go and stand outside my room. You won't be getting out early."

Arthur didn't shout or raise his voice but he did change the tone of voice and was clearly determined in his comments. Dawson got up and left the room. Arthur repeated the question and this time got the expected answer.

"Right everyone, let's all show Mr. Walters how well we can work. In his last school they'd be almost finished by now," said Arthur addressing the class. Children started to look at each other with that questioning expression that, in this case, said "perhaps he's not a new teacher?"

I knew that once again Arthur had saved me from a difficult situation. I later discovered that he hadn't agreed with Ned's decision to give me 2B but that he would not undermine Ned simply find ways to support him or indeed anyone in need. Arthur kept Dawson with him for the remainder of the day, including break and lunchtime and I'm sure made it clear to him that his attitude would not be tolerated because the following days saw a different boy in class. He was no model pupil but at least he was not deliberately obstructive.

I had learned a valuable lesson that day and would always be fully prepared in the future. Lessons needed structure and a variety of activities to stimulate, motivate and interest the children. No more "top of the head" lessons for me, even cover lessons. Confidence was a little slower to develop, but the determination to succeed was something that I had been brought up with. Arthur continued to provide support and advice in the weekly meetings that I had with him to discuss the next week's work; something that he did with all the new staff. I adopted the week ahead approach and tried to encourage other staff to work in the same way. He occasionally popped into a class for a few minutes to see what was going on or to help if he thought there was a problem. At first I was concerned about this, thinking that he thought that I couldn't cope, until I realised that he did this with everyone's classes, including the most experienced of teachers. I will always be grateful for that support and advice which I used throughout my teaching career and hopefully passed on to other staff as I became more experienced. 2B remained very hard work throughout that year. It took weeks of consistent determination to start to win their respect and feel that we were beginning to make some progress. In hindsight it could be argued that Ned was probably right to give me 2B to teach because they certainly helped me to "learn to cope." On the other hand perhaps it was just solving one immediate problem for him.

4

DISCIPLINE.

Learning to cope with classes like 2B, the lack of a permanent timetable at the beginning of the school year and a myriad of other problems seemed to pale into insignifigance compared to building respect among both the staff and the pupils. People say that it takes time to earn respect, which is undoubtedly true, but to an inexperienced, eager to impress and keen to learn new entrant to teaching, time was the one thing that I felt that I did not have. It soon became clear that respect meant different things to different people but within the school the ideas were all related to each other. An example of this came to light only a few weeks after I had started teaching. It was a wet Thursday morning in early October. 2B were being their usual uncooperative selves while we grappled with the idea that the sum of the angles in a triangle was always 180 degrees, when there was a knock at the door. A tall thin unshaven man in a filthy NCB donkey jacket and equally greasy flat cap was stood at the door holding onto a young boy in similar clothes.

"The young' un's been playing the nick. I, I, c, c, catched the little bugger and I, I, I've f, f, f fetched him back," stuttered the man, "he says you're his t, t, t, teacher so I want you to sort it out."

I stood up at my desk at the other side of the room not really knowing what to do or how to tackle this sort of situation. I recognised the boy to be Christopher Hutchinson who, it must be said, had missed a lot of school since the beginning of September, but I've got to be honest I hadn't really noticed that he was missing that particular day and 2B were enough to cope with, without worrying too much about truants.

"Er, perhaps you had better see the deputy head, Mr. P, P, Paterson," I stuttered almost as badly as the tall man had done.

"Paterson, not P, P, P, Paterson, no," stuttered the man his voice louder and the stutter more pronounced.

Just then, as if by magic Arthur appeared behind the stranger.

"Everything alright, Mr. Walters?" started Arthur.

Arthur looked at the tall man and his whole manner, tone of voice, even stature seemed to change.

"Cap off, cap off!" said Arthur sharply to the man.

"Sorry sir, sir, sir," stuttered the man. "Get upstairs and we'll sort it out up there," snapped Arthur.

"Upstairs?" asked the man, a quiver in his voice and the stutter gone.

" Yes, upstairs," snapped Arthur, " and hurry up, and bring young Hutchinson with you."

The man had let go of the boy during the conversation but now grabbed hold of him and hurried out of the room.

Arthur turned his attention to me.

"Could we have a quick word in the corridor, please Mr. Walters? I'm sure that 2B have plenty to be getting on with."

He turned towards the class looked around knowingly but said nothing and slowly walked out of the room.

"Everybody OK, when you've finish try the exercise on page 17," I said to the class, " I'll only be a few minutes and no silliness."

I knew that I was wasting my breath but at least I had tried.

I went out into the corridor.

"So, what's happened?" asked Arthur.

"It seems that Christopher has been playing truant and that man, his father I assume, caught him," I replied.

"Ah, er, alright," said Arthur with a hesitation that was most unusual, "Hutchinson was a pupil here some years ago, he'll expect you, as his class teacher, to cane the lad just as he was caned many times for the same offence when he was here at school."

"Cane the boy?" I asked, " but I haven't caned anyone yet."

In fact I'd been trying really hard to avoid using corporal punishment, although it was still legal at the time and it was used on rare occasions as a last resort in this particular school. I'd heard all the arguments about it being the wrong way to deal with problems and how harmful it could be as well as the "it never did me any harm" brigade but to be truthful I really had just tried to avoid the issue.

"Look, Michael," said Arthur who had sensed my apprehension, "whether you agree with caning or not, caning is the normal punishment for this offence in this school. By doing it you will start to build up some respect amongst both the parents and the children, as long as you're fair about it, consistently firm and fair, never brutal, never done in anger, revenge or haste. Nobody likes to do it, at least no one that cares about the kids."

I listened intently to Arthur. This was a man that I already had the greatest respect for, and he was telling me to cane a child for truancy. I was in a complete quandary, but I knew that Arthur was right in this school and that if I didn't do what was expected I would be making a difficult job into an impossible one.

"But I'm not really sure what to do, how to do it," I said.

"OK," said Arthur, "this is what we'll do. We'll go up stairs together. I'll talk to Mr. Hutchinson, sort things out but I think that he'll expect you to cane the boy. If he does, then you'll have to cane the lad in front of his father. Give him two strokes of the cane, one on each hand. Hit him as hard as you can; aim for the palm and follow through on the stroke. That way his father will be satisfied that you've done the job properly and you'll stand a better chance of hitting him somewhere between his wrist and his fingers. Don't go softly, that's a mistake and will do you more harm than good."

"Hit him as hard as I can?" I asked with a clear tremble in my voice.

"Oh yes, that's most important," replied Arthur, " there's nothing worse than a half baked attempt. Come on let's get it over with."

Before I could think about it, change my mind or do anything else Arthur and I were walking down the corridor towards the staircase that lead to a small upstairs office, built into the roof space at one end of the building. Ned had used this room as his office when he was deputy head but it was rarely used now unless Ned was avoiding someone expected at the upper school. Arthur was a much more involved deputy head, always about and ready to help.

Mr. Hutchinson was pacing back and forth in an agitated state as we arrived at the stairs. The boy was already close to tears.

"Right, up you go," said Arthur to Mr. Hutchinson, who seemed to sprint up the stairway dragging the reluctant boy behind him.

We entered the room, which was very like the staffroom except a lot tidier. In front of the black cast iron fireplace was a large office desk with desk pad and inkwells still in place. Mr. Hutchinson stood in front of the desk shuffling his dirty cap from hand to hand. The boy was now a snivelling heap on the floor. Arthur sat down at the far side of the desk, just in front of the fireplace, which contained a blazing coal fire that kept billowing smoke into the room. I stood at one side feeling awkward and not knowing what to do.

"I must get that chimney swept," said Arthur. "So what's the problem?" asked Arthur with a tone of authority as he looked directly at Mr. Hutchinson. "The little b, b, b, bugger's been playin' the nick again and he kn, kn, kn, knaws I'll get into bother if he keeps deeing it, so I f, f, f, fetched him back to get the stick, to st, to st, stop him," stuttered Mr. Hutchinson. " He can dee it," he went on, pointing towards me, "he's his teacher."

" Would you mind, Mr. Walters?" asked Arthur in a totally different tone to that he had used with Mr. Hutchinson, " it is usual for form teachers to deal with truancy. Give him one stroke on each hand."

"On yer feet, yer little bugger," snarled Mr. Hutchinson to the snivelling child with no sign of a stutter.

The boy reluctantly got to his feet wiping the tears away with the sleeve of his coat. I had occasionally seen other children caned by other members of staff so I thought that I had better try to be very formal and professional about the whole process. Arthur turned to a cabinet on the wall, opened it and handed me a short length of bamboo about a metre long and fifteen millimetres thick. "Right, Christopher, left hand first," I said trying not to be nervous.

The boy stretched out his left arm and opened the fingers on his hand revealing a dirty palm. I followed Arthur's advice and aimed for his palm bringing the cane swiftly and firmly down across his hand. Christopher was clearly taken by surprise, probably not expecting me to hit him as hard. He had been caned before by other staff and knew what was coming. He shook his hand, blowing on the fingers as if to cool them then tried to comfort it by putting it inside his scruffy jacket. It had obviously hurt.

"Other hand," I said.

The boy put out his right arm and opened his fingers. As I brought the cane down towards his palm, he rapidly moved it away. Mr. Hutchinson sprang to his feet.

"You little s, s, s, s, sod, stand up and take your p, pun, punishment," he shouted, clearly disgusted by his son's actions.

The boy looked at his father, stopped crying, stood up and put out his right hand. Swish and it was over.

"What d, d, d, d'you say then?" stuttered Mr. Hutchinson to his son. Christopher stopped shaking his hands and turned to face me directly. I wondered what he was about to say.

"Thank you, sir," said the boy.

Arthur looked at the boy, "You, get back to your class."

Arthur stood up.

" Thank you, Mr. P, P, P, Paterson," stuttered Mr. Hutchinson but he was cut short by Arthur, " Next time, and there'll be a next time, have a bath before you come and learn to control your language !"

"Sorry sir, sir, sir," stuttered Mr. Hutchinson as he made for the door.

He closed the door behind him and started down the stairs. We could hear Mr. Hutchinson talking to Christopher,

"Don't do it a, a, a, again, at least not for a long while or you'll end up getting another dose of the s, s, st, st, stick!"

"Good job there, Michael," said Arthur, "best get back to 2B. Just one thing, don't use their first names, they don't expect it and might take advantage."

I didn't know whether to be pleased with myself or ashamed that I'd hit a child.

As the weeks passed I began to realise that properly administered corporal punishment was not about hurting the child or making them frightened. It was about setting standards of acceptable behaviour, using a deterrent to keep the majority in conformity with only a minute minority ever caned. It was also about expectation and the ethos of that particular school. That particular incident did contribute to a build up of respect that is crucial between teacher and pupil if effective learning is ever to be achieved. It was not about fear, which would have been counter productive, it was genuinely about a sense of respect but at that particular time it did help me to establish an authority of my own which is also an essential ingredient of a good and caring teacher.

It was weeks later before another major incident took a further step towards building my authority, as an individual teacher in school, in the eyes of the children and to my amazement it was instigated by the headteacher.

It was now late November and as seemed to happen in those days it had snowed overnight. There was about 4 or 5 inches of snow in the playground with more piled up in drifts by the walls and towards the entrance to the boys outside toilets. That morning during the first lesson of the day a note was brought round the classes asking all staff to tell the children not to throw snowballs. The note was signed by Ned: this was most unusual and I thought must therefore be important. As luck would have it I was on break time duty later that morning. At the lower school break duty really meant keeping an eye on the children in the playground, keeping the children out of school regardless of the weather – the staff needed a break from the children almost as much as the children needed a break from the staff- trying to stop anyone leaving the premises and watching for bullying or silly behaviour. There was a mixture of age groups on the yard because some of the year 4 and 5 boys had commuted down from the upper school to do woodwork and metalwork as these facilities were not duplicated at the upper school site.

I suppose that it was only a matter of time before the inevitable happened and I realised that I was going to be in the thick of it as a snowball whistled past my left ear. I quickly retreated to the safety of the steps and entrance at the far end of the building where the children normally lined up at the end of break before coming into school. A full scale riot seemed to be going on with snowballs flying in all directions. Amazingly quickly the children had formed several fractions and a real battle was going on. Unbeknown to me, the rest of the staff had heard the commotion and were watching from the staffroom annex window. No one seemed that bothered until the staffroom door was flung open and in stormed Ned having commuted from the upper school, probably to hide from some official visiting from the local authority,

" God, it's bloody card out there," he snorted as he took off a dirty brown coat and shook it into the hearth, oblivious of the fact that most of the dirty water and snow was going all over the staff who were sitting by the fire.

"What's going on out there, then?" asked Ned noticing the staff at the window.

"Nothing Ned, its just……," started Jeff, but Ned was already moving across the room towards the window before Jeff could finish his sentence.

"Whe's on duty?" snapped Ned, "I sent a message down this mornin' about snowballin', I'm not paying for any more broken glass, especially down here," he snarled.

"It's Michael, Michael Walters, Ned," replied Arthur, "we were just about to go out and help him with them."

"Oh, young Wally," said Ned, "don't go out. Jeff nip out and tell Wally to take the names of all them that's snowballing."

Jeff dutifully delivered his message to me explaining what was going on and warning me about Ned being present. He stayed with me to help me with the names of the pupils from the upper school because I still only rarely worked there.

By now much of the snowballing had stopped. Word had spread among the children that Ned was in the building and for most children that was enough: they knew Ned better than I did! However, there's always some who don't listen or don't care or want to build up their credibility amongst their peers, so the list began to grow. As break came to an end, the bell rang and the children lined up at the base of the steps ready to feed into school one line at a time. The list had now grown to 19 children, all of them boys and mostly older boys from the upper school. I was about to start letting them come into the building when all of the lower school staff including Ned appeared in the doorway at the top of the steps, where I was standing. Ned stepped out onto the steps beside me. A complete silence fell over the children who were already reasonably quiet waiting for their turn to come in from the bitter cold.

Ned glared around at the assembled mass and began to speak to them.

" Mr, er, Mr, What's his name, Arthur?" said Ned.

"Mr. Walters, Ned," replied Arthur wondering what Ned was about to do. "Oh, aye, aye, Mr. Walton here will read out the list of you buggers that have been hoying snowballs when you'd been telt not to. You stop where you are when the rest come in!" snarled Ned.

Ned turned to me and said, in a much calmer voice, "Read the list out, then get the rest in."

I read out the list slowly and clearly, then told the other children to start coming into school. There was total silence. In the meantime Margaret reappeared at the door with a cane.

" Right lad, give them two each and look sharp, it's bloody card out here," snapped Ned looking directly at me.

" What two strokes of the cane each for snowballing? And I've got to do it?" I asked, a quiver in my voice.

"Who else?" said Ned, "and it's not for snowballin', it's for disobedience, not doing what they were telt. You're on duty, you whack them, look lively, its card out here!"

I looked at the line of boys, many of them much taller than me. The fear and nervousness must have been written all over my face. A big boy at the front of the queue began to snigger as I walked towards him. Arthur's advice about caning came rapidly back into my head – hit them as hard as you can and follow through.

" Left hand first," I shouted to the queue, intending to go down one side and up the other.

The big lad at the front of the queue put out his left hand. I raised the cane and "swish" it was over. The expression on the boy's face had changed now and he was shaking his hand and struggling to stop tears from forming. He glared at me. Other boys in the line that had also been sniggering desperately tried to look at the boy who had just been caned, craning their necks to see: gradually their expressions also changed.

I moved down the line getting into a rhythm until two boys from the end of the left hand side of the line. The cane snapped as the penultimate boy was caned.

"Don't worry," shouted Arthur, "here's another cane."

Peter Milburn handed me another cane and said,

"Keep going, Mike, you're doing a grand job."

I reluctantly continued the task moving back up the right hand side of the queue. The bigger boy at the front of the queue was not sniggering this time. He stood very still, raised his hand and gritted his teeth. One final "whack" and it was over.

"No more snowballing, you've all heard Mr. Walker's message," I shouted looking down the line of boys, some of the younger one's crying and all shaking their hands in the bitter cold wind that was blowing across the playground, "get yourselves to your classes."

I felt absolutely terrible. But as I walked through the door into the building Margaret said to me,

"What a pro', wish I could whack them like that."

Then Jeff said, "Pretty good, that'll do you no harm in their eyes."

"Canny job, lad," said Ned, "Arthur said you'd a good eye and it saved me the bother, but next time don't let the little buggers chuck the snow in the first place!"

That was probably the closest to praise that I would ever receive from Ned. I didn't realise it at the time but Ned had done me an enormous favour. Not only had the incident established my authority in the Lower School, but it had made an impact on some of the most difficult boys in the Upper School. It had also made a favourable impression on the staff. Now I could start to find other ways of building the children's respect, which I knew was an essential part of the learning process.

5

MISUNDERSTANDINGS.

Its probably fair to say that one of the educational ideas of the 1970's was to encourage children to develop a more questioning approach as they were being taught. It soon became clear that at Alton Grange this "new" approach was not one that would be actively promoted. I now suspect that, with the benefit of thirty odd years hindsight, this was almost certainly the case in many schools and that Alton Grange was probably fairly typical of secondary schools at that time. Of course it didn't feel that way at the time. I actually felt that I had stepped back in time to an era when children were expected to accept everything that the teacher said as Gospel and in many cases this meant taking things quite literally which often led to misunderstandings.

It was common practice among the staff to send pupils on errands during break or at lunchtime. Generally, this was a senior pupil sent for something quite innocuous from one of the local shops. However, like most situations it was open to exploitation by some.

Brian Chapman was another fairly young teacher with three or four years experience. He claimed to have trained as a PE teacher, but he seemed to spend most of his time teaching basic skills to the least able children in years one and two. This wasn't unusual for Alton Grange, after all I was expecting to teach science full time and only had one science class! Brian was a man in his late twenties or early thirties with the attitudes and outlook of a man in his late fifties or sixties. He was a smoker and often ran out of cigarettes during break especially if he'd been free the previous lesson and Ned had caught him. His practice was to send a pupil to buy cigarettes from the ice cream parlour next door to school. However, it was important to select the correct pupil for the task. The proprietor of the ice cream parlour, Alberto Valdesera, was familiar with this practise and didn't question pupils coming into the shop asking for cigarettes for Mr. Chapman. It didn't seem to cross his mind that the cigarettes could be for the pupils themselves or that he shouldn't be selling them to under age people. I'm sure that he genuinely thought that they were for the teacher and he was providing a service.

During morning break on one occasion Brian's supply of cigarettes had once again run out. As usual he planned to send a pupil to Albert's (the name used by the children, and Brian, for the ice cream parlour). Brian called down the narrow, dark corridor from the staffroom to the main corridor to one of the staff on break duty,

" Send 'us someone to go to Albert's."

Margaret Jackson, the geography teacher, was standing in the doorway at the top of the steps leading into school drinking a mug of tea. She looked out into the playground to select a suitable pupil. As she looked around the bulk of the children were just standing about talking or grouped in huddles trying to keep warm in the biting wind, many of them quite inappropriately dressed for the weather. Then something caught her eye. At the bottom of the steps leading to the boiler house she could see a group of second year boys teasing and tormenting a slightly older boy; they were calling him names and pushing him about.

"Here, stop that!" called Margaret, "Leave him alone."

The younger boys backed away leaving a scruffy bespectacled version of the Milky Bar Kid behind them. This was Robert Gregson

– clearly one of life's victims. Robert was in the third year but was part of a special group who were re-taking the second year supposedly to improve their basic Maths and English – a sort of impromptu remedial class.

"Right, Robert," called Margaret, " could you come here for a moment?" Robert got to his feet and reluctantly walked across the yard to Margaret.

"OK, Robert," she said " Go to the staffroom to do a message for Mr. Chapman."

"Aw, do I have to?" moaned Robert.

"Just do as you're told," replied Margaret.

Robert started climbing the steps leading into school dragging his feet on every step.

"Do I have to, miss?" he asked as he passed Margaret at the top of the steps.

"Yes, you do, go on," insisted Margaret.

An equally slow walk along the corridor followed as Robert approached the staffroom door. Just then Arthur Paterson, the deputy head, appeared from the opposite direction; he had been delayed in his room at the end of the previous lesson and was hurrying to the staffroom to grab a cup of tea before the next lesson.

"What are you doing in here, Gregson?" asked Arthur.

"Please sir, I've come to go a message for Mr. Chapman, sir," replied Robert.

His attitude had completely changed. Now he was most willing and hurried to knock on the door before Arthur could open it.

"Gregson for you, Brian," said Arthur as he pushed past Robert and went into the staffroom.

" Gregson?" questioned Brian in disbelief "is that the best she could do?" Brian stood up and went to the door. Smiles grew across the faces of Peter Milburn and Jeff Gray as they listened to Brian try painstakingly to explain his request to Robert.

" Alright, Robert, lad," said Brian.

"Please sir, yes sir," stumbled Robert.

"Good," said Brian "right, go to Albert's and get me twenty Number 6 and if he hasn't got any, anything will do."

Brian paused for a moment.

"Ok, Robert, have you got that?" asked Brian.

" Please sir, please sir, yes sir, replied Robert, "ye want 'us to gan t' Albert's for twenty number 6 and if he hasn't any, just get owt."

"Good lad, Robert," said Brian smiling, " and hurry up before playtime's finished."

Brian turned to come back into the staffroom and saw Jeff and Peter grinning wildly,

"You'll see how all that extra remedial work's paid off," smiled Brian.

"Really, we'll see," replied Jeff.

Robert was running down the corridor but we could all hear him repeating the words, "twenty number 6 or owt" to himself as he ran out of the school doors.

"Its time you stopped all this, you know," said Arthur to Brian. "Its not on sending kids for cigarettes, especially kids like Gregson."

"But Arthur, its good practise for him, going to a shop and taking a message," said Brian trying to justify his actions.

"Remember what happened last time," said Arthur.

He didn't say anymore, he just looked at Brian for a few seconds with a look that said, "you've been warned."

The bell rang for the end of break but Robert had not returned. Staff were reluctantly beginning to make their way out of the staff-room to their classes as Robert came running back to the open staff-room door. The fact that the door was open posed a problem for Robert who did not know what to do.

"Knock, knock," he tried to yell as he struggled to get breath, "A've been t' Albert's for Mr. Chapman," and he thrust forward a brown paper bag.

Brian had just popped to the toilet, which was through a door in an alcove just off the staffroom, and could hear the remarks.

"Take them from him, somebody, please," asked Brian through the toilet door.

Jeff took the bag from Robert.

"Thanks, son, go to your class," he said to Robert.

He looked at the bag. It seemed like an enormous and heavy bag for twenty cigarettes and Jeff's curiosity got the better of him. He opened the bag and burst out laughing. He showed the open bag to Peter who also started to laugh. But before he could say anything Brian emerged from the toilet.

"Here's your cigarettes," said Jeff trying to keep a straight face and holding out the bag to Brian.

"What the……?," started Brian as he opened the bag.

"Well you did say if Albert didn't have the number 6, just to get anything," said Jeff, his voice creased with laughter.

Brian put his hand in the bag and pulled out a bottle of lemonade and a pork pie – probably less harmful than the cigarettes anyway. Everyone roared with laughter. Arthur's laughter gave way to another of those looks that this time said, "see what I mean." I thought that the contents of the bag where quite reasonable since Robert should not have been sent to the shop in the first place. Brian's only comment as the laughter died away was,

"Well at least I've got something for me dinner."

The children's respect for Arthur and his support to all staff were essential for the survival of young teachers starting their careers. He was always about, the children never knew when he might turn up in a lesson, appear in the corridor or just be there when they least expected. He rarely had to say anything and usually let the teacher do the disciplining or praising while he stood silently at one side. His presence helped enormously, especially when dealing with difficult situations, and he went to great lengths to reassure the teacher that him being there was not a sign of weakness or incompetence in the teacher, merely a gesture of support. In those early days he was a Godsend helping us all to solve numerous day to day problems. We were all extremely grateful and I'm sure many of us modelled ourselves on Arthur as our teaching careers developed.

The respect shown to Arthur by the children was probably based on reputation as they came into the school. But as their time in school passed this changed to a respect based on caring, fairness and experience. He was recognised as an excellent teacher encouraging children to leave school with a sense of responsibility and purpose.

However, there were occasions when the respect turned to fear – not a fear of the man, more a fear of the unknown – and this led to several misunderstandings. Arthur was not only the deputy headteacher but also the woodwork teacher; an undoubted craftsman with a real talent for working with wood and respected for it by his pupils. He was seen by them to be the starting point in a career as a joiner, carpenter or cabinet maker – the route to a real job.

Arthur's room was full of the usual paraphernalia of woodwork but unusual in that it had a large open coal fired range set in the middle of the longest wall. An open fire in a woodwork room, Health and Safety would have a heart attack today but at that time it seemed quite normal. I soon learned that the coal fire often received the pupil's work if it was not up to scratch. Of course the traditional fuel for the fire was coal brought in by the caretaker in two large coal scuttles each day from a coal house at the bottom of the yard. However, on one late November morning something had happened to put the caretaker out of his routine and the coal had not been brought in. As the morning progressed Arthur noticed that the fire was burning away and looked to make it up with some more coal; but there was no coal left in either scuttle. 1B, Brian Chapman's registration form was having woodwork at the time. Arthur turned to the boy working closest to his desk, who happened to be Ian Jones; a boy who was new to the area as well as the school and had only been there for a few weeks.

"Stobbart," said Arthur.

The boy looked bemused.

"Jones, sir, Ian Jones," said Jones.

Arthur raised an eyebrow.

"You still look like Stobbart to me, so Stobbart take this bucket," he handed the coal scuttle to the boy, "and fetch some coal."

"Coal?" asked Jones.

"Yes, coal," replied Arthur a little irritated by the boy's response, "you know, that black stuff that we burn on the fire. Go on hurry up before the fire goes out."

Jones looked even more surprised but didn't dare to refuse and scurried out of the classroom.

The door had just closed when it was flung open as Ned stormed in, his raincoat dripping and one side of the collar up while the other was down. "Arthur," balled Ned, "Whe's this ROSLA?"

"Rowlands?" asked Arthur, his back turned towards Ned as he helped a boy with his work. "Is he a new pupil?"

"Nah," squawked Ned, "its another lot of this stuff from County, it keeps gannin on about ROSLA."

"Oh," said Arthur turning to face Ned, " its that Raising of the School Leaving Age, consultation and feedback document. You know we talked about it the other week, but you threw the papers on the fire."

"Aye, aye, but you know Arthur," said Ned in a much calmer quieter voice with just a hint of disgust, "you must be wrong, me throw important papers from County on the fire, you're kidding aren't you? Anyway, this ROSLA kid, which class' he in?"

"No, Ned," said Arthur, "it's an abbreviation, a name for the change in the school leaving age. We'll have to keep the kids for another year."

"Oh, bloody hell," snarled Ned, "I thought it was summit like that."

Without any further explanation Ned spun round, a shower of rain from his coat covering the boys on the front bench, and left the room the door slamming behind him. Within seconds Ned's face appeared at the door again. Through the glass window in the upper part of the door Ned Boomed,

"I'll stop down here for me dinner, Arthur, I'll be in t'office."

Everyone could hear as he thudded down the wooden floorboards of the corridor.

It was now a good ten minutes since Jones had gone for the coal and most people had forgotten all about him, including Arthur. Arthur had to leave his class, who were all busily working in silence on their various woodwork jobs – toothbrush holders and kitchen towel holders for the more able and plant labels for the least able, some of whom still seemed to be making plant labels as they left school but at least it kept the fire going – to go to the kitchen to leave a note for Mrs. Dunn that Ned was staying for his lunch. He usually just did the dinner numbers and then went home, as he lived in the village.

By now it was almost lunchtime and Jones had still not returned. The bell rang for the end of the morning session and as usual the children hurried out into the yard to line up ready to be brought in for lunch. Arthur had completely forgotten about Jones and locked the woodwork room door as he went off to the staffroom for lunch. Most of the staff had just sat down at the table when there was a knock at the door. It was Jones.

"Come in," shouted Peter Milburn and in walked Jones dragging the coal scuttle behind him.

"Ah, Stobbart, where the Hell have you been?" asked Arthur remembering that he had sent the boy for coal.

"Please, sir," replied Jones, " the first six houses I went to wouldn't give us any coal!"

We all started to laugh but Arthur remained straight faced and just looked at the boy.

"I expect that fire's still on next door, Stobbart, that's the one in the woodwork room, not Mr. Valdersera's the ice cream parlour," said Arthur a smile beginning to spread across his face.

"OK," said Jones not really understanding quite what was going on.

"Go and get your dinner," said Arthur and the boy turned leaving the coal scuttle in the doorway as he ran off towards the hall. The staffroom erupted into laughter, including Arthur this time. To this day I doubt whether Jones was aware of his misunderstanding.

He hadn't known about the coal house at the bottom of the yard and hadn't thought to ask anyone. He had jumped over the wall with the empty coal scuttle and gone to the rows of ex-colliery houses behind the school. He had knocked on the doors of several houses and asked for some coal for Mr. Paterson at school. A number of people, possibly ex-pupils squatting in some of the empty houses, had each given a couple of shovelfull's of coal. When he had managed to fill the scuttle he had been unable to carried it back or scale the wall, so he'd had to walk round to the front of the building dragging the coal scuttle behind him.

Just a few days later another example of misunderstanding occurred, again involving Arthur. It was mid lesson and everyone was busy. As usual Arthur's woodwork room was a hive of silent industry, the silence broken only occasionally by the sound of a saw or a mallet as another masterpiece was being created, when suddenly the door burst open and two older boys came into the room pushing what looked like an oversized wheelbarrow.

"We've brung the wood," said the bigger of the two boys confidently.

Arthur looked up from his desk in front of the fire, his glasses perched on his forehead. He said nothing but moved his spectacles into their proper position. "Jackson, Kennedy, in the corridor now, two each hand," he said in a slightly raised voice and a noticeably different tone.

The boys dropped the wheelbarrow and walked into the corridor. Arthur followed behind carrying a cane taken from a polished wooden box hung above the fireplace. The sound of swishing bamboo could be heard along the corridor as the two boys were caned.

"That's one for not knocking on the door and the other for insolence," Arthur explained to the boys.

"But, please sir" said Kennedy, "we've come from Spencer's with the off cuts from the sawmill: we left last year!"

"Oh," said Arthur, "Hmm, well right. Yes, well you know what to do."

"Yes, sir," said Jackson and he carefully took the cane from Arthur and went into the woodwork room where he dipped the cane into a long vase of linseed oil which he then wiped off with a polishing action using the cloth hung near to the vase. He carefully put the cane back into its polished container above the fireplace.

Nothing else was said as the two boys unloaded the timber and left with the empty wheelbarrow. Evidently the school had an arrangement with the local sawmill to take any off cuts of timber for use in the woodwork projects and sure enough Jackson and Kennedy had left school the previous July before starting work at the sawmill. Once again a misunderstanding had led to an unfortunate mistake. There would be no comeback, enquiry or accusations concerning the incident. I doubt whether the boys told anyone back at the sawmills, let alone at home. Probably if they had done they would have looked foolish and may well have been told that they must have deserved it anyway.

It came to light some time later in a conversation with Arthur that he had called at the sawmill a few days later on his way home. He had asked to speak to the boys privately and had apologised for his mistake.

"Must be going soft," said Arthur, "but its always better to admit your mistakes. The kids appreciate that you're only human that way."

We all knew that he wasn't going soft; just doing the right thing and after all it had been a misunderstanding.

A couple of weeks later one of my English lesson's with 1A was very abruptly interrupted by Ned. The door was flung open and he stormed in as usual dragging a little boy behind him.

"This' Philip's he's been bad, he's been in hospital to have some work done on his heart," said Ned, "he's in your class."

" Ok. Mr. Walker," I said. "Go and sit over there, lad," I said to the boy.

" No, no, divent put him there!" screamed Ned, "don't sit him near that hot radiator cos' he's had two plastic valves put in and they might melt!" Another total misunderstanding by someone who should have known better.

6

SCHOOL DINNERS.

Most of us probably have memories of school dinners, but my own now include that added extra – "dinner duty." Alton Grange was no different to any other school in that it had to provide school meals which most of the staff were convinced was the only reason that most children had good attendance. After a few weeks to settle in the new staff were expected to take their turn on a dinner duty rota. The idea was that one member of staff would supervise the children having school lunch each day for a week while the rest of the staff had their lunch break. It meant that you would be on lunch duty about two or three times each term. There was no choice. It was not optional as it was part of a teacher's responsibility at that time.

As newly appointed staff, Arthur arranged the rota so that we would not start doing dinner duty until after the October half term holiday. We would spend a week on duty in the first part of the term with a more experienced member of staff to "see how to go on." I was lucky and was given a reprieve for a few weeks before it was my turn. I word it that way because it soon became apparent that school dinners, or more accurately school dinner registers, seemed to be the most important part of Ned's existence. So much so that many of the children didn't realise that he was the headteacher, they called him "the dinner man." He was fanatical about those meal registers: the way that they were marked; their accuracy and completion. They always took priority over everything else that was going on, no matter how important. For instance, the collection of dinner money on Monday mornings was always personally supervised by Ned and the same sort of performance that I'd been unfortunate enough to witness in the first week was a regular occurrence. The staff had to mark the meals register at registration while they were doing the normal attendance registers and Ned's collection of money had to tally with the register each day. Such emphasis was placed on this task that some staff became quite neurotic worrying that the two figures would balance. I soon realised why!

The staff's anxiety over the school meals money probably stemmed from that initial week of term because from that date onwards Ned alone not only supervised but collected dinner money. Each child entered the staffroom, paid their money and left. Every now and again the silent working atmosphere of the classrooms was shattered by Ned's raised voice as some poor child had forgotten their dinner money or did not have the correct money.

"Forgotten it, forgotten it! How the Hell could yer have forgotten it? If you get no dinner yer'll soon remember it!" boomed Ned at the first one or two children but as the morning went on his patience, if he had any, evaporated.

I often wondered why Arthur went along to the staffroom on Monday mornings at about quarter to ten and stayed until Ned had finished collecting the money. Perhaps it was to check the amount collected or to collect the completed meals registers, but I really think it was to moderate Ned's temper and save the children from Ned's wrath.

School dinners for the staff were a traumatic experience in themselves, not just being on duty. I had imagined the staff being sat at a separate table in the dining hall with the children, but there was no dining hall just a large room in the middle of the building which I thought was the gymnasium because it had wall bars and a collection of PE equipment. It turned out that this room doubled as the hall, the dining hall, a collection point, the gymnasium for the lower school and anything else that anybody wanted to use it for. The staff's lunch was served by one of the dinner ladies and a group of fifth year girls who brought it into the staffroom. The large table at the back of the room having been set by one of the girls who had been dismissed from their morning lessons at about twenty to twelve so that they could commute the half mile or so from the Upper School to the Lower School ready to begin serving the staff meals as soon as the bell rang at noon. It was several days before I realised just how the system worked, where the meals came from (there was no kitchen on the site) who paid for them and so on.

The meals were prepared miles away from the school at a central kitchen that prepared meals for a number of schools in its locality. They were then packed into insulated metal containers and delivered to the schools where they were emptied onto mobile warming trolleys like giant hostess trolleys.

All of this meant that the food had been cooked hours before it was going to be eaten and had been kept lukewarm throughout that time, especially since it was often delivered at about eleven o'clock and the containers stood in the yard outside the main building until half past eleven when the dinner ladies arrived. The result was at best pretty poor but more often pretty bad. Some meals could withstand this treatment better than others – fish was disastrous: the smell was enough to put most people off let alone try to eat it. However, probably the worst meal was a regular which was served within a few days of starting to work at Alton Grange.

It was about twenty to twelve and I was battling to teach 2B maths when there was a knock on the classroom door. Mrs. Dunn the dinner lady was standing at the door. I was quite panic stricken at first, not recognising the checked head square which was about all that was visible through the windows in the door, thinking that it was an irate parent – they were inclined to just wander into school, sometimes directly into classrooms which I'd already seen happen. The door opened.

"Its skilley," shouted Mrs. Dunn across the classroom.

I must have looked a little vacant, so she went on,

"Its skilley for dinner."

"Oh, em, er, OK,"I replied.

She looked puzzled but said nothing and left the room closing the door behind her. Meanwhile groans of "God, Bloody Hell skilley," could be heard coming from the pupils of 2B. I ignored it and continued the battle to settle the class for the last fifteen minutes of the morning session. At last the bell rang and 2B could be dismissed. What was this skilley? I'd never heard of it. I went along to the staffroom and sat down at the already set dinner table. On previous days the rest of the staff had been in the staffroom sat at the table almost as quickly as the bell had rung, but today there was no one. I sat on my own wondering what was going on. A few minutes later the girls who served the staff meals arrived and started putting out dinner plates each having two scoops of mashed potato on them but nothing else. Just then the rest of the staff started to arrive and sat down at the table. Mrs. Dunn followed the last of the girls in carrying a brown paper bag.

" Steak and kidney, Mr. Chapman, mince and onion Mr. Gray," she said and so it went on as she took pie after pie from the greasy paper bag and put them onto the potato clad plates.

As she left another girl arrived carrying a green metal jug with the handle of a ladle sticking out of it. She placed the jug on the table amidst shrieks of "Take it away and what's that smell?" The girl smiled ignoring the comments then left the room. Mrs. Dunn returned before we could do anything. She picked up the jug in one hand and the ladle in the other.

"Skilley, Mr. Morson?" she asked as she pulled a ladle full of the mystery substance from the jug.

"Yes, please," said Rick not really looking at the mixture as it slipped from the ladle onto the plate in front of him. It truly was a disgusting sight; a congealed concoction of indistinguishable vegetables, pale looking minced meat of some kind and lumps of what looked like fat. Obviously, Rick also had no idea what skilley was. We now knew why the rest of the staff weren't having it. Mrs. Dunn's visit to the classroom had been an opportunity to order something else from the baker's in the front street over the road from the school. She would have sent one of the girls across to collect the pies etc. then the staff would pay for them at lunchtime.

At that moment, Arthur came bounding through the door,

" Ah, skilley and you lads having some as well?" he said rubbing his hands together as he sat down at the table.

Before we could answer Arthur set off on an explanation of how good the skilley was, much better than during the war. As an ex – RAF pilot I'm sure he knew what he was talking about but it didn't make the meal look anymore appealing. Both Rick and I would know better in the future.

As the weeks went by it was soon the week before my turn for dinner duty. Arthur suggested that I went along to the hall with Jeff to watch the process and,I suspect, Ned's behaviour. The first couple of days went without any real problems – the children were lined up in their registration classes in the yard, regardless of the weather, in much the same way as they did at the end of break . They were admitted up the steps into school to line up again in the corridor leading to the hall where they were met by Mrs. Dunn who kept order while the duty teacher saw the last of the children into school and moved to the front of the queue. This system allowed the duty teacher to select which class came into school first and was therefore first in the queue to be served. The decision was based on which line was the best behaved or which one was making the least noise or who had gone in first the day before or whatever criteria the teacher chose to use. The children were then allowed to pass into the hall under Mrs. Dunn's supervision and sit at either side of three rows of long trestle tables covered in a ragged green oil cloth: it was clean but had obviously seen many years of service. The dinner ladies stood behind two trestle tables at the front of the hall, the metal canisters of potatoes, cabbage etc., on the table and each lady armed with a large metal spoon or ladle. A large red metal jug stood at the end of the final table closely guarded by one of the fifth year girls: it container the "gravy," a substance whose consistency, colour and smell never changed whatever the meal. The children sat in silence eagerly waiting for their lunch. The cold damp room with paint peeling from the walls, the smell of stale food and smelly wet children made it feel once more like that well known scene from Oliver Twist and I wouldn't have been surprised to hear, " Please sir, I want some more." The duty teacher turned to Mrs.Dunn who nodded when all was ready and the ladies were ready to serve. The teacher then told all of the children to stand and bow their heads while he said grace. Even that act of thanks giving before the meal could be different from the usual, "For what we are about to receive….." to Jeff's "God bless this food and make it good. Amen." The first row of children was allowed to leave their seats, come up to the front tables to collect their cutlery and a plate. They then lined up to have their meal served and return to their seat. The duty teacher's job was to manage the pupil's movements, retaining order and most importantly counting the children. By the time the first course had been served to everyone, Ned or Arthur would usually appear with the dinner registers. This time it was Ned, tightly clutching the registers beneath his left armpit.

"Number," snapped Ned in his usual brusque manner.

This was always a tense moment for the duty teacher, the dinner ladies and even the children who knew all to well what it could mean if it wasn't the number Ned wanted to hear. The number had to agree with Ned's calculation and the response would be,

"Champion, lad" and Ned would disappear without further comment.

So, as I said, for the first couple of days all went well but on Wednesday the numbers didn't tally. Jeff went through the procedure as usual and the children were busy eating their first course. There was a little chatter and harmless banter amongst the children which I thought was quite acceptable and clearly so did Jeff. Ned appeared from nowhere as usual,

"Number?" he snarled as normal.

"Sixty four, Mr. Walker," replied Jeff.

"Oh, Bloody Hell," yelled Ned.

A deathly hush immediately began to spread through the hall. Those children sitting near the front had clearly heard Ned and knew what was about to happen. Their tension spread like wildfire. Ned began checking the arithmetic in the dinner registers. Jeff turned to me,

" Now we're in for it," he said, "keep a close eye on the kids while Ned starts calling out names."

In the meantime the meal continued and the children were served their dessert – a school dinner speciality; cornflake tart and custard. Sure enough Ned checked the figures and as they would not balance he started calling out the names of children registered for free meals.

"1A, free meals, hands up," yelled Ned as he counted the raised hands.

So it went on as Ned went through the classes. Each time that he spoke the slight chatter stopped abruptly into silence, then stated again as Ned looked at the figures in the register. 1A, 1B, 1C, 2A and 2B had all been checked and their numbers tallied with Ned's figures. All the time Ned was becoming more annoyed and irritated.

"2C, hands up if you're paid," Ned went on counting the raised hands.

"2C hands up if you're on free meals."

Suddenly Ned stopped. He had spotted the incorrect number but at that point he did not know which child or children were responsible for the difference in numbers and the possible inaccuracy of the register.

"Right then," snarled Ned, "Everybody stop talking. 2C answer y' names. Ainscough, Brown, Coward, Dobson ….," and so it went on.

The children answering clearly, "Yes, sir" as their names were called. By this time Ned's face was visibly redder and what little patience he had was clearly strained. He had moved to that part of the hall where most of 2C were sitting. Jeff and I had also moved to that part of the hall and we had all three noticed that two boys were talking to each other and had not answered as Ned had called their names. Jeff turned to me but before he could say anything Ned had moved to stand directly behind the two boys who had not noticed him and were still chatting away, their desserts on the table in front of them, spoons in hands ready to eat.

"What's yer name, lad?" snarled Ned at one of the boys.

The startled boy looked round and timidly replied,

"Edward."

"Edward what?" yelled Ned.

" No sir, Edward Franks," replied the boy.

Ned didn't notice the name difference and looked down the list of names in the register.

"And you lad," he said turning on the other boy. " Joseph Crick, sir," answered the boy.

"Free meals, I suppose," snapped Ned as he checked 2C's free meal register.

" Franks and Crick," he mumbled.

The two boys looked at each other and began to giggle. Suddenly Ned yelled,

"Aye , here we are," but then noticed the boys laughing.

Like lightning his left hand dropped the registers, was raised and came crashing down on Franks' left ear pushing his head, covered in a mass of long greasy black hair, down into the bowl of dessert. The follow through brought Franks' head up out of the bowl, custard dripping from his hair. Crick had started to cry at this sight and was clearly frightened.

" Why the Hell didn't yer answer yer bloody name?" boomed Ned.

But before the boy could answer Ned had picked up the registers and was gone. Jeff looked at me,

"Phew, good job he was in a good mood, could have been pretty nasty for a few minutes there."

The silence that had existed during Ned's outburst was abruptly ended and just as quickly replaced with roaring laughter as the children released their tension and laughed at Franks' new custard hair style. Arthur appeared at the door having realised that things were taking longer than usual and wondering about the noise. The children calmed down almost immediately but without the tension that had existed with Ned. It was a salutary lesson in the difference between fear and respect.

It later turned out that 2C was a class of children with a wide range of learning difficulties. Franks and Crick were both pupils with specific learning problems, not least of which was their inability to listen to instructions and concentrate. This did not excuse their inattention but did make it easier to understand. However, special needs was not one of Ned's strong points. At that time it seemed to me that Ned considered such children to be more of a nuisance rather than children that needed more patience and understanding than the norm. This lack of understanding was further highlighted some weeks later when Ned burst into the lower school staffroom, or bottom school as Ned called it, at the beginning of break one morning.

" Arthur!" boomed Ned oblivious to the conversation that was going on.

" Whe's this ROSLA, what class' he in?" he said shaking a collection of pink forms in Arthur's direction.

Ned had been reluctantly going through some old mail from the Local Authority and the DES (the Department of Education and Science as it was then) that had come into school weeks earlier but had been put to one side to be dealt with at the last possible moment. ROSLA – raising of the school leaving age- was hardly a new idea to most teachers but seemed to be new to Ned and just another inconvenience to cope with. Arthur tried to explain in his usual remarkably calm manner, that it was a feedback document following the changes that had taken place and that they had dealt with it weeks before. He was always supportive, calm, respectful and sincere in his dealings with Ned. He was never dismissive with him, or any other member of staff. After listening to the explanation Ned's response was to crumple up the forms and throw them onto the blazing open fire. I was to learn that this was Ned's normal response: that he rarely read anything properly and nearly always relied on Arthur to sort things out.

" If they're bothered, they'll send another lot out to keep the fire going" said Ned, a rare smile on his face.

Without further comment and in a much calmer, less aggressive manner Ned turned away from the fire. Unfortunately this meant that I was sitting directly in front of him. He looked directly at me and said,

"Pour'us a cuppa, lad. I'm the gaffer tha' knaws."

7

PEOPLE

I soon realised that what really went on in school concerned the relationships between the people who worked there. It didn't matter whether it was the teaching staff, the non teaching staff or the pupils. It was the relationship between them that determined success or failure. Alton Grange School was probably very little different to many other secondary schools at that time. It was mainly staffed by ex service men who had gone into teaching following a one year training course after the War. Many of these men were now approaching the end of their teaching careers. The rest of the staff were largely poorly qualified students who had gone to teacher training colleges because they had failed to meet the university entrance requirements. This suited the government of the day as the demand for teachers in the late 1950's and 1960's was a very real problem. To me all of this was an alien world as my background had been grammar school, then a good training college rather than university because I did want to teach and good teacher training colleges were supposed to teach students to teach, or so I thought. But I was beginning to realise that nothing could ever prepare you for the actual job in the classroom.

I had done teaching practices in a variety of schools during my time at college, including a full term in a rural grammar school and eight weeks in a tough Teesside secondary, but the reality of Alton Grange was far different from anything that I had experienced. It was a shock to the system, not just in terms of pupils but the staff as well. My grammar school teachers had not been like these teachers!

I quickly realised that most of the staff were "salt of the Earth" characters committed to teaching and the welfare of the children. I learned to respect many of them and learned an enormous amount from them, but as with all groups of people, their personal characteristics led to many humorous incidents. The headteacher was a classic example; hardly a day went by when Ned wasn't involved in some situation with an element of humour in it. In my opinion, Ned seemed to be a very insecure man, who needed constant reassurance (mainly from the deputy head) and in many ways he was well out of his depth trying to do a job that was far beyond his capabilities. This insecurity showed itself in the many mundane day to day jobs that he insisted on doing rather than delegate them to someone else and which invariably ended in problems. One such job was the collection of dinner money.

Dinner money, school meals registers and free meals seemed to occupy most of Ned's working day. In the 1970's the teacher's unions had just fought for and won improved conditions of service, an example of which meant that they no longer had to deal with dinner money. The consequence was that headteachers had to devise some other way of dealing with school dinners. In Alton Grange this became Ned's principal job to such an extent that he became "the dinner man."

Dinner money problems started on Monday mornings when pupils on free meals had to declare their intention to have free meals for all of that week and pupils paying for meals had to buy tickets for the week. Invariably some children were absent, others did not want meals each day and some forgot to bring their money – sometimes because there simply wasn't any money in the home to bring. All minor problems you might think and easily solved: but not for Ned!

The weekly explosions of Ned's formidable temper usually started about eleven o'clock and could continue until lunchtime or beyond into the actual meal being served. I had witnessed the event several times in the past.

On one such occasion I had the misfortune to be on dinner duty as Ned was trying to sort out the dinner numbers. He followed, a by now, familiar pattern of asking children to raise their hands as he called their names. Then he would count the number of children from each class and hope that the number agreed with the number in the register. The main course had been served as Ned reached the point of no return and bellowed at the children who were chatting quietly as they ate their meal.

"Stop, hold it right there," screamed Ned, his face close to the register and his back to the children, "these bloomin' numbers aren't right."

The usual deathly hush descended on the hall as most children had experienced Ned's dinner number sessions before. Ned turned to face the children,

"Listen, do as you're told an' you'll soon be able to finish yer dinners," said Ned as he started the counting process again.

"1A, Hands up paid meals," balled Ned.

A small group of children raised their hands and Ned counted them.

"Six," he snapped, "check the numbers, Wally!"

I was surprised to hear myself being called "Wally" by the headteacher but I later discovered that this was actually a good thing and a nickname was usual for Ned if you were being accepted. I obediently did as I was told, probably because Ned wasn't the sort of person that you would disobey.

"That's right, six, Mr. Walker," I replied.

Ned continued to work his way through the classes while I provided a double check. Each class dutifully responded until we reached 3C, the last class. Throughout the procedure Ned had gradually become more irritable and less patient as he was still unable to find the culprit to the incorrect number.

Just then music started to fill the hall; a single trumpet or a French horn perhaps; something brass anyway playing a slow soulful melody. Everything stopped, including Ned, as we all looked around wondering where the noise was coming from. The music suddenly stopped and a raised voice could be heard coming from the cupboard at the end of the hall. Ned stormed across the room and flung open the door. He stood still staring for a moment,

"What the Hell are you doing?" he shouted.

All of the children were craning their necks trying to see what was in the cupboard but no one dared to move, including me. From the corner of my eye I could see a young lad holding a battered brass cornet and a little old man in a shiny black suit.

"Oh, its you, Barnes. Come on, get out, get out! Time I went for me dinner." Ned stormed off out of the hall forgetting all about his precious dinner numbers and everything else; his thoughts were now firmly focused on "his dinner."

Everyone breathed a sigh of relief as Ned left the room knowing that for the moment the tension and uncertainty had gone but could be back later in the afternoon when Ned remembered the incorrect numbers. Meanwhile a bewildered Mr. Barnes was speaking slowly and calmly to the boy with the cornet, the two of them still cramped up in the cupboard doorway. This was not the raised voice heard earlier, more like that of a concerned grandfather figure. Mr Barnes was an incredible sight; a small frail man, clearly in his seventies or older. The black suit immaculately pressed but with a shine that said that it was well used, and a matching waist coat and pocket watch. I was struck by his black boots, one having a patch neatly stitched into the side just at that point where your foot bends. He was a smaller version of my own grandad, which made me feel some empathy for his situation.

"Good afternoon, sir," said Mr Barnes as he walked past me towards the staffroom, pulling his pocket watch from his waistcoat pocket, "didn't realise the time."

"Hello," I replied awkwardly still wondering quite who this old man was and what was going on as the boy with the cornet ran past almost knocking Mr. Barnes off his feet.

"Steady, lad," said Mr Barnes.

By now the rest of the children had returned to their meal and almost all of them were ready to start queuing for dessert: the famous tapioca.

"Oh, God! It's frogs spawn," said Jacqueline Atkinson in a loud voice clearly heard above the clatter of plates and scrapping knives.

"Oh, ah," was the general opinion but they all collected their bowls and sat down looking pretty miserable as they ate it. Once again it reminded me of the gruel sequence in the musical version of Oliver Twist .

The practice was for the teacher on duty to wait until the last child had completed their meal, check that everything was OK with the dinner ladies then go to the staffroom to have their lunch. The staff had their lunch in an annex in the staffroom, with meals brought in by a team of older girls; it was considered to be quite a prestigious job to " wait on the teachers at the bottom school." Most staff had finished their main course and were about to tackle the tapioca, but they all seemed to be waiting for something. I'd learned by now that it was sometimes a wise move to say nothing and watch the situation unfold.

"Are you finished, Mr. Barnes?" asked Brian Chapman.

"Yes, thank you young man," replied Mr. Barnes.

"Champion," said Brian, "can you pass the dessert?"

The tapioca had been delivered to the table in a large metal jug. The frail old man tried to pick it up but from his sitting position obviously found it too heavy to lift. Mr. Barnes made several attempts to lift the jug and was clearly embarrassed by his efforts. Brian started to laugh and I then realised that the whole episode had been set up to ridicule the old man. I picked up the jug and passed it along the table.

"Don't do that," sniggered Brian, "Mr. Barnes' in training, you're ruining his programme."

But no one laughed. Perhaps they could all see the silliness of the situation and the puerile behaviour that Brian had shown.

However, two weeks later I was to witness the same scenario; this time with a large jug of custard being passed again by Mr. Barnes at Brian's request. It would seem that Mr. Barnes was a victim of Brian's sense of humour or perhaps it was more like an example of bullying an elderly person. The old man didn't get annoyed but I'm sure that he was frustrated by the events. He had a respect for teachers that had long gone and in some cases was not deserved. He called everyone sir and always waited until last to be served at lunchtime. He would stand in the staffroom at break until everyone else was seated.

It turned out that he had been the band leader of the local colliery band and when he had retired at 65, years before, he had been asked if he would like to tutor some children in brass instruments. So he'd agreed to tutor but the contract had just kept on going. I doubt whether anyone at staffing in County Hall realised how old he was.

Mr. Barnes said nothing for the rest of the lunch break but as staff were beginning to leave for their afternoon classes he turned to me and said,

"He's a card, Mr. Chapman."

But I wonder what he was really thinking. That's not to say that Mr. Barnes was some saintly old man. Many times over the following months those raised voices were heard coming from the cupboard and they were not always young voices raised in frustration. I soon realised that Mr. Barnes could be firm with the children even if he found some of the staff more difficult to deal with.

My dad always treated everyone the same; it wouldn't have made any difference whether they were royalty or just someone he'd met in the street. I suppose that I am much the same, and although I know that other people very definitely place people in a hierarchy it came as quite a surprise to see this sort of discrimination so frequently in teaching. To me the teachers and the non-teaching staff were all just workers doing a job but to others a gulf existed between the teachers and the rest of the staff that could not be crossed. I suppose that one of the things that concerned me was that if a gulf existed at that level how could the distance between teacher and child ever be overcome.

I realise that a certain distance is necessary but if it's too great I doubt whether much learning can go on.

At Alton Grange, the hierarchy was very clear cut. Mr.Walker, Ned, the headteacher, was in charge (or so he claimed) with Arthur as his right hand man (really in charge). Then came the teachers and finally the non-teaching staff – secretary, dinner ladies and caretaker. The caretaker was a bit of a mystery because he hardly ever seemed to be about during the school day. I used to think that he must be stoking the boilers of the old coal fired cast iron central heating system until I realised that it had been converted to oil – this was the era of "coal cleansing" especially in a village that had just lost its coal mine. However, like many school caretakers, even today, he did seem to spend much of his time in the boiler room. He did however emerge from its depths to complete a daily ritual for most of the year, certainly October to May – lighting the open fire in the staffroom and taking it out of the grate before school ended! This meant that anyone not teaching towards the end of the day couldn't work in the staffroom or even sit in it for that matter; our refuge was removed.

The situation and the mysterious activities of the caretaker was made worse that winter because unknown to anyone else he had decided that he would use the labyrinth of rooms off the boiler house, formed in the cellars beneath the classrooms as part of his latest money making scheme. We later discovered that he was growing mushrooms in the dark, damp conditions of the cellar and selling them to a local market trader. None of the other staff were aware of Jack's business. Unfortunately one of the essential ingredients was a medium on which to grow the crop and he had chosen to use well rotted horse manure.

Everything came to light one Friday morning in early March. The caretaker had arranged for a delivery of the potent mixture to arrive the previous day. It was delivered by a coal merchant who worked in the village but still delivered using a horse and cart. The manure delivery was obviously a side line to solve the problem of the rotting waste. However, the delivery had not arrived until late the previous evening and Jack had not had sufficient time to move the foul smelling substance into the old bread trays in the cellar where he was to grow the mushrooms. His solution was to move the manure into the boiler house over night, presumably to complete the move the following day. He had given no thought to any possible odour permeating through the building.

That morning we all arrived for work as usual but the staffroom fire wasn't lit and there was no sign of Jack. Jeff was first to arrive, having been dropped off at the lower school by Arthur Johnson who he travelled with and I arrived shortly afterwards. It was bitterly cold and damp in the room, which did not benefit from the central heating in the rest of the building. I started to lay the fire from the bundle of sticks and old newspapers kept under the table by the caretaker. The first thing I'd noticed as I walked into the building was the smell; not the normal smell of damp or stale school dinners but a much stronger more pungent smell.

"What's that smell?"I said to Jeff.

"Must be Dowson. I expect Margaret kept him back last night and forgot to send him home," laughed Jeff.

Dowson was a little boy in the first year who had been "stitched in" for the winter. (this was the practise of wearing the same clothes throughout the winter months, often sleeping in them and not changing them. I understand that in the thirties it was quite common and children were quite literally stitched into their clothes by sewing the clothing together, but this was the 1970's and this little lad was a victim of the pit closure. His family were squatters living in the old, no longer considered habitable, colliery houses that formed rows at the bottom of the school yard with the original names of "First Street, Second Street etc., up to Eighteenth Street." Dowson did wear the same clothes throughout the winter, possibly because they were the only clothes that he had, and undoubtedly slept in them as the family tried to keep warm by burning all of the wood in the upstairs of the house; the doors, architraves, even the floorboards, on the open fire. When all the wood had been burnt they moved on to another house. There was no running water or electricity which must have made it difficult to keep clean). Dowson did smell through no fault of his own and he was by no means alone but this was a different kind of smell and Jeff was just trying to be funny although we both knew that the little boy's situation was far from humorous.

As more staff arrived almost everyone commented on the smell, some instantly looking at the soles of their shoes. Margaret Jackson was probably the most disgusted by the smell and, little did we know, the most accurate in her description of "smells like a herd of horses have run through here." Just then Arthur came into the staffroom. He'd been busy in the woodwork room when I'd arrived and I hadn't noticed him – he was a real craftsman and sometimes made items of furniture in his own time for customers as a bit of a money spinner.

"Morning, all," said Arthur.

"Arthur," said Margaret, "the smell, what're we going to do about it?"

"What smell?" replied Arthur.

We all looked at Arthur.

"Yer Kiddin'," said Jeff.

"No, no what smell, I can't smell anything," said Arthur, "Anyway its probably something outside. It's about time we had them in. Peter ring the bell."

The bell rang and the children started to line up ready to come into school on Peter's instruction. As they filed in and started to move along the corridor it wasn't long before the comments started and the faces were pulled, but Arthur just ignored it and went off to his room. Registration passed with a lot of moaning and comment about the stench which seemed to be getting worse as we went into the first lesson and before long it was morning break. The children went out into the yard behind the school supervised by Peter as it was his break duty day. The staff hurried to the staffroom, some desperate for a cigarette or a cup of tea, but all complaining about the smell. Break was almost over when Simon Bateson came through the door.

Simon mainly taught PE at the upper school but had been told to cover an English lesson at the lower school and had walked down during his break. "What the Hell have you lot been eating down here," he said as he came into the room and noticed the smell.

"Very funny," said Margaret. "See, Arthur, even Simon's noticed it!"

"Ah, Simon," said Arthur, "you've got 3C for English next lesson in room 6." "Oh, God," responded Simon, "not 3C, what'll I do with them?"

"Get them to write a story," suggested Brian tongue in cheek knowing that most of 3C had trouble writing their names let alone a story.

"Look," said Arthur, "read them a story, anybody got anything suitable?"

I had just finished reading a short story called "The Left Slipper" with 2B who weren't much better than 3C but had seemed to enjoy it, so I said,

"Here Simon, you could try this" and I passed the book across the room. "Thanks," said Simon as the bell rang.

We all moved off to our classes, mostly still complaining about the smell.

Room 6 was a spare room seldom used except when someone was ill and Arthur preferred not to use that person's classroom for cover. It was in a pretty poor condition with paint peeling from the walls where the dampness had taken control as water poured through from the roof. The furniture was a complete mix of all the oddments and damaged pieces from other classrooms. Children did not like this room which always meant trouble if you were on cover. It was also positioned directly above the boiler house making it uncomfortably hot at any time of the year.

Simon stood in the corridor outside room 6 waiting for 3C to arrive. Peter had kept them outside until the rest of the children had come in from break so that he could give the room change to them on their own to try to avoid confusion. Simon could hear the groans about room 6 and the smell as the children came into school, then it suddenly began to change as the children saw Simon standing at the door. Simon was a bit of a heart throb for many of the girls in school and a role model to the boys. He had been a professional football player before injury had forced him to leave football and move into PE teaching. He was still a young good looking man.

"Are we doing PE with you, sir," asked Nicola Waites a wry smile on her face.

"Just get inside," replied Simon as the children filed into the room. Within minutes they were all back out in the corridor moaning and groaning, some coughing and spluttering as the smell in the room was unbearable. We could all hear from our classrooms further up the corridor.

"Go and get Mr. Paterson, George," said Simon to a tall boy in the line, "ask him to come to room 6 as soon as he can."

The boy went off to find Arthur and the class became more restless in the corridor. Arthur arrived within a few minutes looking rather puzzled,

"What's the problem, Mr. Bateson?" he asked.

"Just step in there for a minute," replied Simon pointing into room 6.

Arthur went into the room, looked around then returned to the corridor.

"A word, please, Mr Bateson over here," said Arthur with something in his tone that showed his displeasure.

"Look, I know it's a bit of a mess, Simon, but its only for one lesson," started Arthur, "you'll just have to make the best of it. Settle them down, start the story and most of them will go to sleep anyway."

"But the smell," said Simon, "we can't …"

Arthur broke in, "What smell? Everybody's going on about a smell. I can't smell anything."

Simon shook his head in disbelief but told the class to go back into the room. The children reluctantly started to move back into the room, still commenting on the smell under their breaths. Arthur stood at the front of the room, arms folded (not a good sign) while Simon started to read the story. Within minutes the class was settled and seemed to be listening to the tale. Arthur left and returned to his own class.

By lunchtime the smell seemed to be beginning to fade, or perhaps we'd just got used to it, and there was still no sign of the caretaker as we sat down around the table in the staffroom waiting for the meal to be served. Brian Chapman came in and immediately asked,

"Where's Simon?"

Brian had probably been going to torment Simon about his cover lesson with 3C but Simon wasn't there.

"I'd better go and find him," said Brian and off he went down the corridor.

A few seconds later Brian returned trying hard to control his laughter.

"You'll have to come and see this," laughed Brian, "but quietly."

We left the table and quietly went down the corridor to room 6, the smell increasing in intensity as we approached the door. Looking in through the corridor windows we could see all of the small class sprawled across their desks asleep. Sat at the teacher's chair with his feet up on the desk was Simon also asleep.

"Shall we just leave them?" whispered Brian.

"Don't be so stupid," said Margaret who unusually had not gone home for her lunch. "We'll have to wake them."

She opened the door to go in but was almost knocked back by the smell. "God, its awful in there, where's Arthur?" she said.

Arthur hadn't been in the staffroom when Brian had made the initial discovery but was now striding down the corridor.

" What's going on down here?" asked Arthur in a loud voice. Loud enough to wake some of the children who had been sleeping in the classroom.

"Look at this lot," said Margaret "and the smell in there's unbelievable. If you can't smell that then it's time that you went to the doctor's."

She was probably the only person that could have spoken to Arthur in that way, having known and worked with him for years. Arthur's head dropped,

"Enid's been going on at me about going to the doctor's about it, I suppose I'd better. Anyway, these kids, we'd better let them go. It's lunchtime."

Arthur opened the door and Simon woke up with a start,

"Everything's alright, Mr Paterson," spurted out Simon quickly putting his legs off the table. The staff all began to laugh and Simon looked puzzled. Arthur sent the children off to lunch. By now the smell was invading the corridor quite forcefully.

"We'll have to do something about this smell before this afternoon," said Margaret.

Arthur looked at her and said to everyone,

"I'm sorry you've had to put up with it this morning, I simply can't smell it. I'll see what I can do for this afternoon but we'll just keep it to ourselves for the moment, not mention it to Ned. Anyone seen Jack?"

We all agreed that it would not be a good idea to inform Ned but no one had seen Jack, the caretaker.

Arthur set off to find Jack while the rest of us returned to the staffroom for lunch. About ten minutes later Arthur appeared at the staffroom door, a broad smile on his face.

"Did you find Jack?" asked Jeff as Arthur came through the door.

"Oh, yes," said Arthur, " and the source of the smell."

" So what was it?" questioned Jeff.

"Well let's say, it'll soon be gone. What's for lunch?" Arthur wouldn't be drawn on the smell issue and simply said that it had been dealt with.

The rest of the day was still fairly smelly but it had definitely faded as the day went on. Arthur still wouldn't give anything away and the caretaker still hadn't been seen. Most people probably thought that he was ill. At least it was Friday and perhaps by Monday everything would be back to normal.

The following Monday I arrived at school to find a blazing fire in the staffroom hearth and Jeff making the tea. The room now smelled of bleach but at least the appalling smell of the previous week had gone. It was weeks later before Arthur explained what he had found that Friday when he had gone looking for the caretaker. It turned out that Jack had started to move the manure from the boiler house but had stopped for a rest as it was heavy work and he had also fallen asleep. Arthur had found him sat on a pile of the foul smelling substance, pitchfork in one hand and his pipe in his mouth the rest of the room full of the rotting manure. Arthur wouldn't tell us what he'd said to Jack but the manure and everything else was gone. Jack was very subdued, possibly grateful that he hadn't lost his job and obviously grateful that Ned hadn't been told. He was much more helpful from that time on.

Months later Arthur went into hospital to have a polyp removed from his nose; the result of years working in the dusty atmosphere and sawdust of the woodwork room. His sense of smell seemed to improve after the operation.

8

WINTER

Many people are affected by the weather. It changes their view of the day, their mood and the way that they respond to other people and situations. I don't suppose that I'd ever really considered how big an impact the weather could have on people and particularly children until I started teaching. Ask almost any teacher and they'll moan about the effect of the wind on the mood and behaviour of any group of children. It was certainly the case at Alton Grange. The problem was made worse by the split site and the need to commute classes of children between sites. Added to this was the uncertainty of whether the commute would actually take place because if the weather was too bad, children remained wherever they were and the timetable was adjusted to accommodate the situation.

The winter brought with it the extra problems of snow and ice. There were however, some lighter moments that made up for the general mood of depression. One such episode became known as "the snow trousers."

It was mid December, not long before the end of the first term and the weather was bitterly cold with frequent, often heavy snow showers. There were a few inches of snow lying on the ground and as one batch began to melt another shower would replace it and add to the accumulation on the roads and pavements. So the level of snow varied from day to day, but what made it even more obvious was Ned's regular visits to the bottom school.

Ned usually wore a black or very dark navy suit, which he seemed to wear most of the year. Being a fairly short stocky man, his trouser legs were always right down to the ground and in fact seemed a bit too long for him. Ned was meant to be stationed at the top school where he had an office and secretarial help but he regularly came down to his old haunt at the bottom school where he had been deputy head for many years or if he was trying to avoid anything official such as a visitor from the Local Authority. He would "work" in the upstairs office and during the winter in particular he often told Arthur to tell the caretaker to light the coal fire. As mentioned earlier Arthur rarely used the office.

It was midway through morning break when Ned arrived flinging open the door in his usual manner and almost knocking the mug of tea from Margaret's grasp. He flung his dirty dark brown overcoat across the room towards an empty chair and made for the roaring coal fire to warm himself up having just walked down from the upper School.

Jeff nudged my arm,

"Look at the trousers," he said.

I watched and listened as Ned held court in his normal manner ignoring anyone else's conversation. Nothing seemed to be happening. I looked at Jeff trying to work out what he had meant, then Ned turned around to face the fire. The back part of the lower section of his trousers, just above shoe height, which had been wet from the snow had started to dry out in the heat of the fire. As they did a white tide mark caused by the salt from the road started to form part of the way up the trouser leg showing the depth of the snow. The salt from the footpaths and roads that he'd had to cross had dissolved in the snow water and was travelling up the material of the trouser like a chromatography experiment, forming it's own chromatogram. I smiled at Jeff, who was trying not to openly laugh.

"Notice how high it is today," Jeff said almost in a whisper, "bet it's even higher tomorrow."

Ned didn't notice what was going on and I doubt if anyone else did but the next day I couldn't wait to see how the tide mark had changed or whether Ned would have realised and changed suits.

As expected Ned did his usual and arrived half way through morning break. Jeff and I were keen to see the new snow mark without being spotted. Ned went through his ritual of warming himself in front of the fire while holding court or talking to Arthur but this time he didn't turn around. We couldn't see whether there was a mark or not. Jeff was leaning over Peter who was sitting next to him, trying to see Ned's back.

"Watch what you're doing," said Peter.

Jeff backed away pretending to have picked something up from the floor. It was looking like we would not be able to tell whether there was a mark, when Peter saved the day by offering Ned a cigarette.

"Here Ned, try one of these," Peter said.

Ned wasn't going to turn down a free cigarette so he moved from the fireplace across the room to take the cigarette from Peter. Jeff glared at me gesturing to look at the bottom of Ned's trousers. Sure enough there was yesterday's white line, now quite distinct and obvious but above it a new line was beginning to form. I looked across the room at Jeff and raised my eyebrows in recognition of the new level.

Throughout that winter Ned wore that same suit; the series of white tide mark lines varying with the depth of snow or the volume of rain. No one told him about the marks although I suspect everyone noticed. He was a more accurate indicator of the weather than the weather forecast. So the snow trousers were born.

The winter weather caused all sorts of problems but also had its funny side, especially when commuting between sites. On one occasion it revealed yet another facet of Ned's amazing behaviour. The bottom school staff often heard Ned recount tales about taking one of his lady friends out for a meal: he fancied himself as a bit of a catch! He always concentrated on what they had eaten and the meat in particular. There was never any detail about the lady despite a lot of questioning by Margaret and Arthur. He was definitely not a vegetarian and I'm sure that he thought that vegetarianism was an illness. This point was vividly brought home after watching Ned collect his meat order from the butcher's opposite the bottom school every Tuesday afternoon, usually just as we were about to commute between sites.

The example in question took place towards the end of the first term. I was coming out of the gates of the bottom school with 1A who were going to the top school for PE when we noticed Ned's car across the road parked outside the butcher's. The road was covered in ice and hard packed snow and was extremely slippery. We all knew that it was Ned's car immediately because of the cigarette ash. Ned drove a brown Mark 1 Ford Escort at the time and it was literally full of cigarette ash and spent matches. The nasty stain on the back seat was the result of a broken bottle of milk that Ned "had not got round to clearing up." We were just crossing the road as Ned came out of the shop carrying some parcels of meat neatly wrapped in white paper. He must have seen us quite clearly but there was no acknowledgement or comment as he negotiated the pile of snow that had been pushed into the gutter by the snowplough earlier that day. He stumbled and almost fell as he climbed up the mound of snow while trying to find his car keys at the same time.

The children also noticed what was happening but weren't sure whether they should laugh or not.

"There's the dinner man," said Tony Eales pointing towards Ned, "is he gettin' our dinners, sir?"

"No, No, Tony," I replied. "Come on, hurry up, get over the road before a car comes," I continued trying to make light of the situation.

But Ned was struggling with the slippery road, his car keys and his parcels of meat. One parcel slipped from beneath his arm and a string of sausages fell into the snow.

"Oh bugger it," yelled Ned putting the rest of the parcels on the car roof while he bent down to pick up the sausages.

By now people were stopping to watch the spectacle. Suddenly a Jack Russell terrier appeared from nowhere, picked up the sausages and ran off down the road as fast as it could.

"No yer don't. Bloody dogs," balled Ned and he gave chase careering along the slippery snow covered pavement of the Front Street behind the little dog, his brown overcoat billowing out in the wind like a cape.

"Stop that dog, it's nicked me sausages," we could hear him shout as he ran off into the distance.

The children from 1A had continued to walk while this had been going on and had nearly reached the point where they would meet up with 3C commuting from the top school to the bottom school for art. The idea was that the two teachers would exchange classes and return to their respective work places. Both groups of children had witnessed the incident and were rolling about in laughter. I must admit to smiling myself but I had to try to remain serious and try to restore order.

"Come on, keep going," I shouted, "stop at the pedestrian crossing!"

As we arrived at the crossing we were met by Ned coming back towards his car. He had a white parcel with two sausages hanging from one end, held high above his head in one hand. The little dog was barking madly around his ankles as Ned coughed and spluttered, trying to light a cigarette with the other hand. Ned said nothing. I looked across to speak not really knowing what to say but Ned just walked past, the dog still snapping at his heels.

We crossed the road and reached the change over point about half way between the two sites. Ned's car went slowly past struggling to grip the road surface on the slight gradient in the road. But the thing that caught everyone's attention were the white parcels on the car roof. Ned had obviously forgotten that he had put the parcels on the car roof and in his hurry to escape the Jack Russell he had driven away without moving them inside the car. What to do? Did I simply change classes and return to the bottom school or should I hurry up to the top school to tell Ned about his extra roof load? I thought for a few minutes then I shouted across the road to Madeline Watson, the teacher that I was due to change classes with,

"Will you keep an eye on 1A while I run up to tell Ned about the parcels on his car roof?"

Madeline glowered back at me, which was not unusual and I took it to be a yes. I ran as best I could on the slippery surface up the hill to the top school arriving as Ned was getting out of his car. Without saying a word Ned got out of his car, slammed the door shut and picked up the parcels from the roof. He started walking across the yard towards his office completely oblivious of what he'd just done. I didn't know what to say but didn't need to as Ned announced,

"What's the matter, lad? Got lost?"

"I, er, I, " I began but was interrupted by Ned.

"Did you see that bloody dog nick me sausages?"

He obviously didn't want a reply because he had continued to walk pushing through the door and into school. I was left feeling a bit stupid, then I remembered Madeline and I thought that I'd better hurry back to the change over point. I tried to explain what had happened but Madeline didn't want to know and just walked away in disgust. I hurried back to the bottom school with my new charges, an unruly class known as 3C who were to cause me problems later in the year.

The cold weather also highlighted the poor living conditions of many of the children. Many were inappropriately dressed, some without coats, lots still wearing their summer sandals or shoes, both completely unsuitable for the weather but all that they had to wear. I suppose that I must have been a bit naïve and I did not realise quite what was going on until a number of incidents occurred that helped me to understand.

The first incident came to light as I was calling the register one Friday morning in the middle of winter.

"Robert Newell," I shouted.

"Here, sir," he replied, "and we've shifted houses, again."

"Alright, Robert, stay at the end of registration and I'll make a note of your new address," I said.

Robert waited until the other children had gone off to their first lesson. He was small for his age, very shabbily dressed and he had a peculiar smell about him: not a dirty, soiled clothing smell or body odour smell but a smell that I began to notice more and more on the majority of children over that winter. It was the smell of stale food that lingers on clothing hanging in the place where food is being cooked and for many of these children the kitchen was probably the warmest place in the house.

"14, First Street," said Robert, " we'll probably be there for a few days."

I wrote down the new address and must have looked a bit puzzled as the boy went off to his class.

The following Monday I was again calling the register. As I came to Robert's name there was no reply.

"Anyone seen Robert Newell this morning?" I asked looking around the class.

"He's shiftin' today," replied William Maddison.

"Is he? Where's he going? Do you know?" I enquired.

"Wherever there's some wood left," said William, looking at me as though I was a complete idiot, "probably's up Eighth Street," he went on.

Trying not to look anymore of a fool I thought that I'd better leave it with the children and sent them off to class.

At morning break I caught Arthur on his way to the staffroom. As we walked along the corridor I thought that I'd mention the Robert Newell situation.

"Ah, yes," said Arthur, "young Newell's dad was a good lad when he was here. He worked at the pit but when it closed he was left with nothing, like so many others. There's a lot of them move house very regularly when the weather's cold. They're squatters mostly; they burn all of the wood in one house to keep warm then they move to another house as the wood is burnt. Just keep a note of his address changes if you can keep up with them."

I was amazed. I had never heard anything like it.

Later that week the plight of some of the children was further highlighted when I inadvertently overheard part of a conversation between Margaret and the mother of a boy in the first year.

"They might fit your Philip," said Margaret handing a carrier bag of clothes to the woman.

"Eh, thanks very much, Mrs. Jackson," said the woman, "I'm very grateful, things are that dear and they grow that quick and Billy's still got no work."

She was close to tears.

I looked at Margaret but said nothing. She was trying to be discrete and I'd interrupted. I quickly hurried out of the way. I had heard Margaret talk about her own sons. These were probably clothes that they had grown out of and no longer needed. It turned out that the school held jumble "sales" on an almost monthly basis, organised by Margaret as a sort of clothes exchange – I'm pretty sure that no money changed hands. The children all seemed to accept it. There was no envy or jealousy, no "I'm not wearing that!" no having to have new clothes all the time and certainly no sign of designer clothing!

There were many other incidents that further helped me to understand the situation at Alton Grange. Two more of them, occurred that winter and both of them could be attributed to the state of the school premises. The first was a very unfortunate experience for another young member of staff, Bob Simpson who had joined the staff part of the way through that first winter beginning at the start of the second term, as his first teaching post. He was travelling to school on his own at the time and had just bought a new car. It was a Citroen Dianne – a sort of up market Citroen 2CV it seemed to me. Bob was obviously very pleased with it and proud to be its owner. However, one morning towards the end of January that all changed.

The school yard sloped quite steeply away from the main school buildings, making it very difficult to park on in icy weather. On this particular day it had been very cold the previous night and the yard was covered in a thin layer of ice like a skating rink. Bob pulled into the yard, applied the brakes but nothing happened. The wheels locked but the car continued to slide down the hill and crash into the wall at the bottom of the yard – it simply crumpled into a heap of twisted metal.

We heard the noise from the staffroom and looked out in dismay unable to do anything. Bob climbed out of the mangled wreck unhurt but unable to believe his eyes and struggling to keep on his feet on the almost glasslike surface. There was nothing to say, but everyone made their sympathy clear.

The following day the incident was almost repeated: this time by an oil tanker.

The school had only recently been converted to oil fired central heating. This conversion to oil was going on all over the county as more and more coal mines closed and it was obvious to all that a decision had been made that this was the end for coal. The oil level was monitored by the school caretaker who then had to estimate when to order new supplies of oil, a job that the caretaker, Jack, found very difficult to do and in fairness it must have been difficult to make that judgement as there was none of the electronic gadgetry of today. Jack checked the oil level in the large delivery tanks with a marked piece of wood never looking very confident that he knew what he was doing.

All of that January had been bitterly cold with frequent icy weather and a biting northerly wind. There had been some snow, which was hard packed on the ground. Jack checked the oil on Wednesday and thought that he'd better order a delivery to last the next few days and over the weekend – hence the oil tanker.

The tanker driver pulled into the school yard and because of its sloping nature began to brake. Immediately the vehicle began moving towards the scene of Bob's impact with the wall. Somehow the driver managed to control the lorry and ended up parallel to the wall. A very white faced man in a navy blue boiler suit jumped down from the lorry's cab.

"You've had it for your oil," the driver shouted across the yard to Jack, who was stood watching from the warmth of the doorway to the boiler house.

"I canna' get to the tanks, it's too risky, they're too near that wall," he went on. Jack said nothing just shook his head and went back into the boiler house closing the door behind him.

Somehow the oil tanker driver managed to turn his vehicle around in the larger part of the playground away from the wall. With a lot of wheel spinning, rocking the vehicle backwards and forwards, to say nothing of the swearing, he managed to drive the tanker out of the school yard.

The rest of the week saw the weather gradually deteriorate so that by the weekend it was very cold with frequent prolonged snowfall. The journey to school the following Monday was horrendous as drifting snow had blocked the road in several places and although some of it had been cleared by snowplough it was only wide enough for one vehicle to pass. Gingerly we made our way to work taking much longer than usual and finding it difficult to keep warm. As we arrived at school it was clear that something was wrong. There were children running away from school, their faces beaming and the shouting and laughter could be heard even with the car windows closed. We turned into the school yard to be met by Arthur telling another member of staff to go home. It would seem that the oil supply had run out on Saturday morning. With no heating over the weekend and the severe icy conditions, several pipes had burst. There was still no oil supply although a delivery was expected later that day, but then there would still be the frozen pipe problem. So there was nothing for it but to close the school. We were to be sent home until we were contacted that school could reopen. This was excellent news to the children and almost as well received by the staff: an excellent feeling, an extra "holiday." I don't know who was the most pleased the staff or the children. What was even more amazing was that the same problem had occurred at the top school which had similar access problems and the driver who had been meant to deliver at the bottom school should have then delivered oil to the top school as well.

So both premises were closed. Ned was in a real flap but there was really nothing that he could do and for once it wasn't directly his fault. The situation took a turn for the worse later that week when the oil delivery was made. The obvious bursts had been repaired but when the heating was eventually fired up numerous new leaks were discovered in the antiquated cast iron heating systems in both schools. It was six weeks before both schools were reopened and back to normal. During that time only the children in year 5 had any teaching using a couple of rooms at the secondary school in the next village.

There were no complaints from parents, no undue hassle from the Local Authority, just an acceptance that it was an unfortunate incident caused by the winter weather. There didn't appear to be anyone held accountable for the loss of schooling. The winter had certainly made its presence felt.

9

HONESTY

In a school were most children had few material things jealously was always going to be a problem showing itself in minor pilfering from each other or occasionally stealing from the community. The school was seen as the overall authority in the community setting standards and maintaining the unwritten rules. Looking back with the benefit of hindsight it seems to me that parents were much more in control of their children than they are today but they relied on the school to support them at times that would otherwise have involved the police. Several times during that first year the close links between parents and school or the community and school, would be put to the test. Today we still talk about that three way partnership of pupil, school and home expressing it as "a new idea." It isn't new. It's always been there, except that thirty years ago it wasn't just talked about, it actually worked.

One family in the village operated a coach tours business and had children who attended the school. This is probably being very generous since it was really a fairly run down concern running old service buses from a galvanised steel shed completing school runs and the odd day trip. "Lamb's Luxury Coaches" was struggling to survive like most other businesses since the pit closure. The coaches had seen a lot of service but I assume that they were still road worthy and we did use them if we were going out of school – not that visits to museum's and the like were common- so it was especially annoying for Mr. Lamb when one boy in year three developed a liking for stealing buses, driving them about for a while then leaving them miles from anywhere. This had happened several times and although the police had been informed their involvement had been minimal and the boy had not been caught although it was common knowledge who was involved.

In desperation, I suspect, Mr. Lamb came to school to ask for help. As another former pupil, it can't have been easy to come back into school. However, Arthur was always willing to help and listened to Mr. Lamb's predicament.

"We could hold a line up," Arthur said to Mr. Lamb, " we'll line up all the older boys, you can walk down the line and just point out any that you think are involved."

"But I haven't seen the boy," said Mr. Lamb.

"Oh that doesn't matter," replied Arthur, "just look out for any that might be a bit shifty, watch their eyes and the amount of fidgeting that that they do."

I was surprised to hear this. It sounded more like something from a television programme rather than a secondary school but I have to admit having used the same technique effectively many times since.

The boys were rounded up and told to form a single straight line in the yard. Mr. Lamb walked along the line looking carefully ay each boy. When he came to the end of the line Arthur said,

"Anyone then?"

"I'm not sure," replied Mr. Lamb, "there's one or two shady looking lads among this lot!"

" That's certainly true," said Arthur becoming a little irritated, "but coach stealing. Anyone?" Mr. Lamb pointed at John Barrow, a small curly haired boy in year three (about 14 years old). Arthur looked directly at Barrow.

"You, go straight to my room," said Arthur.

Barrow looked at Mr. Lamb then back to Arthur. "I didn't nick them buses," said Barrow.

"Just go to my room, lad," repeated Arthur.

Barrow took one more look at the two men, turned and ran off across the playground at high speed heading towards the high wall at the bottom of the yard.

"Shall we fetch him back, sir?" said two much bigger boys who were stood further along the line, their question directed towards Arthur.

"Yes go and get him but don't hit him unnecessarily, I need him alive," replied Arthur shaking his head.

The two boys set off at great speed, scaling the wall as if it was nothing.

"Looks like we've got a suspect," said Arthur to Mr. Lamb, "do you want me to call the police and contact his parents?"

"No, no, no....eh, you can deal with it, please," replied Mr. Lamb.

"But it really should be the police, it's stealing, driving without a licence and all sorts of other offences," said Arthur.

"No police," said Mr. Lamb, "they're bloody useless and he'll only get away with it."

"Hmm, just as you like," said Arthur clearly not very happy with the situation.

A few minutes later the two boys were back carrying Barrow between them. He was kicking and screaming but seemed to be unhurt. Being much bigger than Barrow the two boys simply held him down.

"Thanks boys," said Arthur as they dumped Barrow at his feet, "don't think about running away, lad, or the two whippets will be after you again! We'd better go up to the office," said Arthur to Mr. Lamb. The staff who should have been teaching the other boys were all stood outside watching the events unfold.

"Get this lot in, please Mr. Blackburn," said Arthur, "and everyone back to class. Anyone not teaching at the moment?"

Peter Milburn and I were both "free" but Peter said that he would keep an eye on Arthur's class and he was expecting a delivery of metal, so Arthur turned to me.

"Just pop upstairs to witness this, will you, it won't take long."

I'd heard this expression before and had a good idea what was coming ,or so I thought.

" Of course," I said not knowing what else I could have done.

Meanwhile Barrow and Mr. Lamb had made their way to the office. I think Barrow had given up on the thought of escaping knowing that plenty of his "friends" would be only too pleased to drag him back. As I entered the office the two characters were stood together but it was difficult to tell who was the most nervous – that office clearly brought back memories for Mr. Lamb. I stood to one side of the room. Arthur came in and sat down at the large desk in front of the fireplace.

"Right, let's get this over with," he started, "Barrow do you admit stealing one of Mr. Lamb's buses?"

"Coaches, luxury coaches," interrupted Mr. Lamb.

"Er, yes, coaches," repeated Arthur with a frown.

Barrow didn't seem to be quite with it; in a sort of daze. There was a short pause.

"I just took it for a little drive," said Barrow, " I didn't do any harm or anything."

"Didn't do any harm!" yelled Mr. Lamb, "is that why it ended up in a ditch?" He lurched towards Barrow who backed away but Arthur was already on his feet standing between the boy and the furious Mr. Lamb.

"Let's calm things down a little," said Arthur sitting down again, "so you definitely took the coach, Barrow?"

The boy nodded.

"Right, well punishment," said Arthur.

"He needs a good hiding," started the now extremely annoyed Mr. Lamb, "if I was his father I'd."

But he was stopped in his tracks as Barrow yelled,

"You're not me dad. I haven't got a dad!"

Arthur stood up again,

"Right, right, never mind all that. I should really just call the police and let them deal with it but Mr. Lamb has insisted that I deal with it. I'll have to cane you and write to you're mother about this stealing business. You'll be getting two strokes on each hand, left hand first."

Arthur reached into the cabinet on the wall and brought out a cane. Barrow put out his left hand. Whack! Barrow fell to the floor nursing his hand and screaming,

"Fetch the police, I want the police to come, I'm not having anymore."

Throughout this episode I'd been standing rather awkwardly by the doorway watching and listening to what was happening.

"No police," yelled Mr. Lamb.

Arthur looked directly at the boy who was already a little less agitated,

"OK I'll telephone the police and Mr. Lamb, here, can insist that you're charged with stealing the coach. You'll probably end up in an approved school or an assessment centre or something this time……. it'll be hard on you're mam, but if that's the way…"

Before Arthur could finish, Barrow was back on his feet, tears gone, the drama over. Arthur finished the punishment. This time Barrow didn't flinch. He was obviously used to much worse and as tough as old boots.

Arthur opened the drawer of the desk and pulled out an official looking book, rather like a register but with a well worn cover.

"I'll have to enter this in the official punishment book, Barrow," said Arthur, "with the reason for the punishment given as 'stealing a coach'."

Mr. Lamb's face changed from anger to anxiety as he heard the words 'punishment book' and 'official entry'.

"Thank you, Mr. Paterson," started Mr. Lamb, "I'm very grateful that…" Arthur interrupted him and stopped any further comment by saying,

"Perhaps we should ring the police and report the stolen coach anyway?" But before there was time to reply Mr. Lamb was out of the door and clattering his way down the stairs.

Barrow was looking at Arthur not knowing what he was going to do.

"It was a silly thing to do, lad," said Arthur to the boy, " no more, mind. Go back to your class."

The boy seemed to have taken the caning in his stride and his little outburst was obviously an attempt to avoid further punishment. Barrow left the room and Arthur said to me,

"Sorry that you had to witness that, but it's always best to have a witness for something like that. Mr. Lamb's not the easiest of people to deal with. I blame his parent's for saddling him with a Christian name like that. Shaun that is."

I looked puzzled, then it dawned on me: Shaun Lamb. We both began to laugh, but in fact that really was his name.

It was almost Easter and time seemed to be dragging when the next example of that three way partnership between school, community and parents was put to the test again.

The Lower School was a very old building; it had been suggested that it was formerly the Workhouse, built directly in the Front Street of the village. The playground and the children's toilets were at the bottom of the yard behind the school leading towards the lower edge of the colliery waste tip (the pit heap) and some rows of houses previously owned by the colliery. These houses were now in a state of serious disrepair and many housed squatters, the long term unemployed and a small number of life long residents. They formed a large part of the school's catchment.

The school was surrounded by shops on either side and directly across the road. At one side of the school was an ice cream parlour run by an Italian family under the direction of Alberto Valdesera. This was not unusual at the time as most pit villages seemed to have an ice cream parlour, which had been the haunt of the 1950's teddy boys of blue suede shoe fame. Many of these establishment's were still in business struggling to make a living probably more on cigarette and sweet sales rather than ice cream specialities such as knickerbocker glories and banana splits. Mr. Valdesera was well known and respected in the village. The children tended to talk about "Albert's" but not in a disrespectful manner. However, that relationship almost broke down following an incident one afternoon break: an act of dishonesty on a large scale.

The ice cream parlour was adjacent to the school but the buildings were not joined together. The shape of the school was such that it narrowed at that point leading to a gate in the boundary wall with the Front Street. This made the playground much bigger in that area and its boundary was the gable end of the ice cream parlour. High in that gable end was a small window. Through the glass the word "Mars" could be seen on the sides of boxes piled next to the window. This was the trigger for an incident that the staff were oblivious to until later that afternoon.

It was almost the end of the day when Albert (Mr. Valdesera) came rushing into school demanding to see Ned. Arthur heard the commotion and came out of his woodwork room into the corridor. We could all see and hear what was going on through the thin glazed panel walls separating the classrooms from the central corridor: Albert's raised voice and Arthur's calm but firm reply. "Where's a Ned?" screamed Mr. Valdesera his English tainted with an Italian accent, "I need to see Mr. Walker."

Of course Ned was no where to be found, and in fairness he didn't "work" on the Lower School site, not that Mr. Valdesera would have been aware of Ned's promotion to headteacher.

"Ah, hello Mr. Valdesera," said Arthur his glasses perched high on his forehead, "what's the problem?"

"They'va stolen my chocolata," shouted Mr. Valdesera, his moustache twitching and plainly in an agitated state.

He was dressed in a spotlessly clean white jacket in contrast to Arthur's brown dust coat.

"I'm sorry, what exactly has happened?" asked Arthur puzzled by the angry comments that were making Mr. Valdesera's accent even more difficult than usual to understand.

"Ned, he is here, yes?" said Mr. Valdesera in a slightly calmer manner.

Arthur tried to explain that Ned was now the headteacher and worked at the Upper School. Meanwhile the school had fallen completely silent as everyone, staff and children listened carefully to the exchange.

"Come, come, you come," said Mr. Valdesera taking hold of Arthur by the sleeve.

The two men walked along the corridor and out into the playground. In school the silence was broken by Margaret's voice,

"Just get on with those notes on Africa, I've just got to pop out for a moment," could be heard while Jeff's firm controlled tone was heard to say,

"Finish those questions on forces and no noise," as the door to the science room opened.

Meanwhile in the playground Arthur and Mr. Valdesera were having quite a conversation accompanied by a lot of hand waving and pointing from the Italian, much of it directed towards the little window high in the gable end of the ice cream parlour. Then almost as quickly as it had started the voices stopped. Mr Valdesera walked back across the playground in the direction of his shop and Arthur returned to the school building. We all listened intently as Arthur spoke to Margaret, who was now standing in the doorway,

"They've been stealing sweets from Mr. Valdesera's, it would seem," said Arthur, "somehow they've managed to get in through that little window in the gable end. Mr. Valdesera's really annoyed, and rightly so. I suppose I'll have to inform Ned. There'll be Hell on."

"Can't you deal with it, Arthur?" replied Margaret, "I'll keep an eye on your class. Don't tell Ned. You know what he's like!"

I hadn't really worked out the staffing structure in school and needless to say no one had thought it necessary to explain, but it seemed that Margaret was a sort of senior mistress, responsible for the girl's welfare at the Lower school. She had worked with Arthur and Ned for many years.

"Do you really think so?" asked Arthur, "I suppose Ned'll only go crackers. Right, we'd better have them all in the hall and I'll talk to them. I'll send a runner round with a note."

The silence in school began to beak. A murmur could be heard moving around the children in the classrooms. It wasn't possible to clearly distinguish actual words but something was obviously going on. About five minutes later a boy knocked on the classroom door.

"I've fetched this from Mr. Paterson," he said handing a piece of paper to me through the open door.

The hand written note simply said, "Please bring your class to the hall as soon as is convenient. Thanks. A. Paterson."

"OK son, thanks," I said to the boy.

"Can I have the note back, now," asked the messenger.

" Yes, em, er, thanks," I replied handing the paper back and turning to face the class who were all silent, anxiously waiting to find out what was officially going to happen.

"We need to go to the hall and line up as you do for assemblies," I said.

Within a few minutes all of the children were in the hall talking noisily amongst themselves but there was no sign of Arthur. The minutes passed and staff tried to quieten their charges. Then Arthur appeared at the back of the hall. There was an immediate silence as he walked towards the front of the room. He looked different. Then it dawned on me. There was no brown dust coat and his glasses weren't perched high on the forehead of his balding head. He was wearing a navy suit and looked the model of authority, far more so than Ned had ever done.

The children said nothing as Arthur began to speak. There was no shuffling, no fidgeting or movement of any kind and definitely no talking. He spoke in a slow, calm clear voice. It was not raised or angry simply that of authority and complete control.

" I had a visitor this afternoon," said Arthur, " Mr. Valdesera from the ice cream shop next door. He was very annoyed because he had just discovered a break in. Someone had stolen a large number of chocolate bars and a variety of other sweets. I was very surprised and suggested that he informed the police immediately. But Mr. Valdesera seemed to think that some of you might know something about it. Does anyone know anything about it?"

Arthur looked around the hall. No one moved. No one said anything. The silence was eerie. The lack of eye contact, as children looked down or away, was very obvious.

Arthur continued to scan the hall for a few seconds that felt like hours, then said,

" Well that's a relief. That's what I thought, nothing to do with us. Don't you think so, Dawson?"

Arthur moved forward among the children until he was standing directly in front of Joe Dawson.

"Empty your pockets, lad," said Arthur looking directly at the boy.

"I've nowt in them," protested Dawson with a snigger on his face.

"Good, then you won't mind emptying them. Just empty your pockets, son," said Arthur his tone of voice having changed slightly.

He didn't sound angry or annoyed just more determined. Reluctantly Dawson pulled some items from his pocket: a short folding knife with a four inch extremely sharp and dangerous looking blade, "his pencil sharpener" he said; a cigarette lighter, "just looking after it for me dad," he claimed; and a half eaten Mars bar. The rest of the children looked on in silence.

"Where'd you buy the chocolate?" asked Arthur.

"Can't remember," replied Dawson turning to look around the rest of the children, a grin on his face.

Arthur picked up the remains of the Mars bar still in its wrapper.

"They're all numbered, these," said Arthur, "Mr. Valdesera will have the batch numbers written down for stock control purposes. We'll just send this next door to establish whether its one of his stock."

"Please yoursell," jeered Dawson , "its nowt to dee with me."

Then very quickly Arthur snapped back at the boy,

"And what about the cigarettes, that's a police matter!"

"Didn't take any tabs," said Dawson with panic in his voice.

" So you were there," said Arthur, "but you didn't steal any cigarettes?"

" I wasn't there," snapped Dawson, the grin had now gone and been replaced by a worried look as he realised that he'd fallen into the trap, "it wasn't me. Tony gave us the Mars bar. He must've nicked it!"

Tony Young was a boy in year 4 with a real attitude problem, a terrible reputation for bullying younger boys and a very unpleasant manner.

"You lying toad," yelled Young at Dawson, "we all know it was you and the kids that are too scared of you. Wait till I..."

Young started to move towards Dawson but Peter Milburn caught hold of him by the arm and escorted him from the hall still shouting and swearing about what he was going to do to Dawson.

The whole incident had lasted only a few minutes. Everyone had witnessed it, everyone had listened to the exchange and Arthur's skilful handling of the situation. I had seen a technique being used which I was to see expertly used in exactly the same way time and time again over the years, and one which eventually I would use myself.

"Right, the rest of you with chocolate, hand it over," said Arthur looking around the hall.

The next response was not at all as Arthur had imagined. It was quite unbelievable watching as the majority of the children started pulling chocolate bars from their pockets, bags and belongings, both boys and girls. The children piled the sweets on the table at the side of the hall. What we had all thought was a minor theft turned out to be a major robbery. Arthur was clearly not amused.

"Now the cigarettes and anything else that you've taken," he yelled in an uncharacteristic voice.

A group of mainly older boys stepped forward squabbling amongst themselves about whose fault it was that they had been caught. No one tried to deny the theft or argue in an attempt to get away with it.

The children returned to the places where they had been standing. Silence returned as the shuffling and squabbles ended. Everyone's attention was focussed on Arthur. He looked directly at a boy in year 4 called Christopher Brass.

"Brass," said Arthur, "I want you to tell me what happened, in your own words."

Arthur scanned the hall, "And I want the rest of you to say nothing. Not a word, whether you agree with Brass or not. There will be no interruptions, gestures or movement of any kind. Does everyone understand?"

Arthur made another obvious scan of the assembled children.

I don't know why Arthur had singled out Brass. He was another difficult boy; often in trouble and regularly on the periphery of any incident but not often the instigator of the problem (perhaps I've answered my own question). In reality he was probably one of a group of boys who had a better relationship with Arthur than they had with other teachers. He could teach them a skill that they could really understand and see as relevant to their prospects when they left school – woodwork and prospective joiners, carpenters and cabinet or furniture makers. Brass tried to explain what had happened.

The incident had occurred at afternoon break. Breaks tended to be a bit flexible as the weather improved. It wasn't unusual to hear Margaret say to Arthur,

"We'll just give them a few more minutes, Arthur, they're looking a bit pasty. The sunshine'll do them good, plenty of vitamin D."

I wasn't really sure what she meant, or whether it was tongue in cheek, or was she just trying to give the staff an extra break or perhaps there was some other reason.

Brass stumbled his way through his story. The rest of the children stood in silence and listened intently. He explained how some of the children had seen the words "Mars and Cadbury" on the sides of boxes visible from the window in the gable end wall of Mr. Valdesera's shop. The temptation had simply been too much. Arthur stopped Brass at this point.

"That's no excuse," he said, "the sweets were not yours to take. It is stealing and should be reported to the police. But one thing puzzles me: that window must be about twenty feet off the ground, how did you get in?"

Brass smiled,

"That was the easy part. A couple of weeks ago some of the young 'uns went to a RAF motorbike thing with Mrs. Jackson. They saw the display team riding round like a one of those pyramid things all on each other's shoulders. We thought we could make one of them pyramid things and get Titch to climb to the top and open the window."

Titch was the nickname for Michael Harbottle, a boy in year 4 who had some sort of growth problem making him probably one of the smallest boys in school. Brass continued to explain,

"So we all piled up on each other and Titch climbed up to the window. The wood was all rotten and that, so he just pushed on it and the glass fell out. Then Titch opened the window and climbed in so that he could hoy the tabs and that out. We telt him to hoy some kets out for the kids to stop them grassin' us up. Titch went crackers like and chucked all sorts out. It was raining kets. Everybody was pickin' them up."

Arthur gestured to Brass to stop again and began talking to the whole assembly,

"Well that explains why so many of you stupidly got involved. By picking up the sweets and keeping them you've made yourselves as guilty as the actual thieves."

He turned his attention back to Brass.

"You've explained the sweets but what about the cigarettes?" he said.

"Like I said, Titch went daft and was chucking everything out the window and someone shouted up to see if there was any cigs. When he found them he chucked them out as well."

"You said someone shouted," said Arthur, " this is important, the sweets are one thing but the cigarettes are another matter. So who was behind it?"

Brass dropped his head and started to fidget. He was obviously uncomfortable but he knew that Arthur meant business and was not prepared to let go.

"It might have been, er, I think it was Tony Young," mumbled Brass not daring to look up.

Immediately the words, " Grass, grass, grass," were being chanted loudly by a group of older boys near the back of the hall. Arthur glared at them and the noise stopped as quickly as it had started.

Arthur looked back towards all of the children.

"Anything else anyone would like to tell me before I deal with this?" he said firmly.

"What about the stash in the toilets?" said Alison Burnell, a girl in the first year, in a very timid voice.

"You stupid pillock," could be heard coming from several children from all directions in the assembled mass.

"Would you like to go and bring them in?" said Arthur in a much calmer tone realising that this little girl had no idea what she'd just done.

"Can Jody help me?" asked Alison, "there's too much to carry myself."

Arthur nodded and the two girls ran out of the hall, the glaring faces of many children starring at them.

By now it was almost the end of the school day. Arthur spoke to the hall full of children,

"Its nearly home time, but this isn't over, not by a long way. We'll sort it out in the morning. I want everyone back here first thing in the morning whether you're meant to be here or not. I'm going to ask your teachers to take the names of all of you that were involved. Be honest, remember we all saw you put your hands up when I asked you about your involvement before and I know that most staff were very busy writing down names then!"

The children were sent back to their classes and an air of relief could be felt but they all knew that tomorrow the punishments would be handed out. They all seemed to accept and understand that they had done wrong and that doing wrong had a penalty to pay.

My own class had about two thirds of its children involved. I was disappointed and wanted them to know. I started to talk to them,

"Taking something that doesn't belong to you is stealing. That makes most of you thieves. I'm bitterly disappointed in you."

"God, it's only a bloomin' Mars bar," said Brian Williams.

"It doesn't matter what it was," I snapped back, "it was stealing. And one Mars bar? There were dozens of them. Well Mr. Paterson will deal with it in the morning."

"What'll he do?" asked a white faced Sharon Giles, "he'll not tell me dad, will he?"

"I don't know," I replied, "we'll find out in the morning. Time that you were going home. You might think about what you've done and whether you should tell your parents yourself."

The bell rang for the end of the day and the class was dismissed. Sharon Giles hung around as the children filed out. She was close to tears.

" Don't tell me dad, please don't tell me dad," she pleaded, "I'll get such a walloping if you do!"

"I don't know what will happen Sharon," I said, "you'll just have to wait until tomorrow."

Sharon left in tears. I felt some sympathy for her but she had taken the sweets like so many others.

With the children having left the building the staff collected in the staffroom. This was most unusual because it was normally a race to see who would leave first: a "Le Mans" style exit from the car park most nights. But this was different and we all wanted to know what Arthur intended to do the following day. I suppose that we were trying to support him for once.

Arthur was last to arrive.

"The little buggers," he said, "I've never known so many to be involved in something like this," and before anyone could comment he added, "so this is what I think we'd better do."

Arthur explained that if it had been an incident involving one or two children he would have told them off, possibly they would have been caned and certainly their parents would have been informed and they would have been made to apologise to Mr. Valdesera. However, with this number of children involved that wasn't possible. Instead he wanted each form tutor's help. Each child that was involved was to write an apology to Mr.Valdesera offering to replace the stolen goods. It would also tell Mr. Valdesera that they would be expected to tell their parents what they had done and that they would be kept in detention after school for an hour each day for the remainder of the week. Detentions were very rare at this time in this school and seen as a real punishment by the children. Bearing in mind that it was Tuesday, that meant three hours of detention or as the children saw it, three hours of torment. It was assumed that all form teachers would do this and as everyone wanted to support Arthur no one questioned it.

To be honest the whole thing was being dealt with so well, without any hesitation or questioning about what to do, that we were all glad to help. The cigarette thieves would be dealt with separately. Arthur told us that Mr. Valdesera didn't want to involve the police because he thought that the children involved would just get away with it and he knew that school was more likely to find the culprits and punish them. Arthur said that he intended to ask Mr. Valdesera to come into school to witness their punishment or involve the police at that stage if he wished. If Mr. Valdesera continued not to involve the police, the boys would be caned by Arthur in his office as well as doing the detention for two weeks, which he would supervise, a letter would be posted to their parents informing them of their part in the robbery and the punishment that had been given and the boys would have to write the apology. Arthur finished his explanation and apologised to the staff for keeping them and expecting them to supervise the detentions but he pointed out that by being seen to work together we would be sending out a clear message to the children on the subject of stealing and of course he was right. His final words were,

"And by the way, we'll keep this to ourselves, no need to bother Ned."

The following day children arriving at school were not in their usual high spirits. They moped about in the playground or huddled in groups waiting for the bell to go. There wasn't even the kick about that was always going on. When the bell rang they lined up in silence and were very quiet as they filed into school and down the corridor to their form rooms.

Each form teacher had to explain to their pupils what was going to happen. I expected a backlash or counter argument but there was silence. Then Sharon Giles raised her hand.

"Will you help us to write it properly?" she asked, " we are all sorry and we know that we shouldn't have taken the sweets."

"Of course I'll help you," I replied, "first lesson's been delayed by twenty minutes so that we can sort it out. So what do we need to say in this apology?"

A sea of hands went up and more children tried to contribute than you would ever find in a lesson. They seemed genuinely to be sorry and wanted to make that clear to Mr. Valdesera. Gradually we managed to word an apology, which I wrote on the blackboard.

"This will be our first task tonight in detention," I said, "to make a neat copy of this apology."

The rest of the week was most peculiar. All of the children seemed subdued and there were no complaints about detention. Arthur investigated the incident fully identifying the instigators and those children involved in the cigarette theft. Mr. Valdesera was invited into school on Thursday morning to witness their punishment as he still refused to have the police involved.

The final detention on Friday night was just about to start when a girl knocked on the form room door. She was acting as a messenger for Arthur and brought in a note asking all form teachers to take their forms to the hall immediately. A buzz went around the class as I read out the message. Everyone wondered what was going on – had Ned found out and what would the consequences be if he did know? We went along to the hall in a state of both trepidation and excitement and waited for the deputy head to arrive.

After a few minutes Arthur arrived accompanied by Mr. Valdesera. The hall fell silent. Arthur spoke to the assembly,

"I've brought you all together to put an end to this matter. I've explained to Mr. Valdesera how sorry you all are and assured him that an incident like this will never happen again."

There was a long pause as Arthur made a deliberate scan of the hall, his eyebrows raised above his glasses. Arthur went on,

"Mr. Valdesera is satisfied that you have been suitably punished and has accepted your apologies. He is being very forgiving and wants everyone to make a new start."

Mr. Valdesera was smiling and nodding as Arthur spoke. Then two men in the familiar white jackets commonly seen in Mr. Valdesera's ice cream parlour appeared at the back of the hall carrying large shiny metal canisters. A young girl, also in a white jacket that was clearly too big for her, followed them carrying a cardboard box. The children remained silent but were obviously curious. Arthur spoke again,

"The end of this matter is a very generous "gift" for each of you from Mr. Valdesera and his family: you will take it and leave the hall quictly."

Mr. Valdesera, still beaming, said,

"Its'a my besta ice'a cream'a. You all'a take one, yes. You can'a all come back to the shop'a, anytime, but you no take'a the sweets!"

He shook his head and pointed his fingers in the air with the final words.

The two men at the back of the hall started handing out ice cream cornets to the children as they left the hall and went home. It turned out that during that week none of the school children had gone into the ice cream parlour and this had had a dramatic impact on the takings. This couldn't go on but a point had to be made. It was also another example of Arthur's excellent judgement and experience and his standing in the community.

The following Monday Ned arrived to collect the dinner money as usual but his opening words were,

"Here, Arthur, they tell me you've gone cuckoo, buying all the kids an ice cream."

"Not quite, Ned," replied Arthur concerned that the real truth was about to come out.

"There was a bit of bother but, er, we sorted it out," he continued.

"Right, champion," said Ned, "I thought they'd got it wrong in the Club. Giv' us a tab, Peter."

Ned turned his attention to Peter Milburn who handed over the cigarette. Arthur smiled and looked around at the staff. No one said anything but we were all thinking the same thing. Ned as usual was completely oblivious to the real issue.

10

TAKING THINGS LITERALLY.

It soon became apparent that as a teacher you had to be very careful about what you said to the children. Many children were unable to read between the lines, interpret messages or signals, or make inferences and simply took things quite literally. This regularly led to misunderstandings or outright mistakes.

Matthew Brown and Ian Simpson were experts at taking instructions literally, on the odd occasion when they were actually listening, and this often landed them in trouble. On one particular occasion they caused quite a problem by misunderstanding a notice.

It was Monday morning and Ned was ensconced in his regular Monday position having a cigarette while collecting the dinner money in the staffroom during the first lesson of the day. I was covering Peter Milburn's absence looking after 3C who were supposed to be doing some Maths. 3C were probably the least able of the children in year 3, many of them having learning difficulties and effectively making them a remedial class. The major concession was that groups like this were a bit smaller at around 25. Most of them could not focus on a task, had very limited concentration spans often accompanied with behavioural problems, so they were always going to be a handful. The dinner money collection was normally a nuisance, breaking the flow of the lesson, but on that morning I was glad of the break from the metaphoric head banging.

Matthew and Ian were good friends who sat together near the front in the middle of the class; an indicator that they probably weren't usually too much trouble. They left the room with the rest of the class when it was time to sort out their dinner money and ended up at the end of the queue. Both boys were on free meals so there shouldn't have been any complications. The boys gradually moved up the queue and into the staffroom while Ned marked the dinner register, collected the money and allocated tickets to the children. He was having a "discussion" with a boy from 2B as Matthew and Ian stood in the middle of the staffroom.

"Look, lad, I canna' do nowt about it. If yer mother's got nee money 'til Thursday, you've got nee tickets and nee tickets means nee dinner, right. That's the way it is!" snapped Ned, "tell you're idle father to get himself out of bed and find some work!"

More words of wisdom from Ned.

However, while all of this was going on, Matthew and Ian were looking around the staffroom as they warmed themselves in front of the coal fire. They were oblivious to Ned's conversation with the other boy but fascinated by the layout of the staffroom and the things in it. They noticed the cups and kettle, the large glass ashtray full of cigarette ends and spent matches as they nudged each other and pointed things out. Then Matthew's attention was drawn to a notice on the wall pinned to the NUT board. Like most staffroom notice boards this one was not properly organised, in fact a real mess. Each organisation or department was supposed to be allocated a particular space and this area had been given over to the teaching union, the NUT. But someone had pinned the notice in question in that NUT space incorrectly. It was a list of names under the heading 'Suggestions for a new class' and of course both Matthew and Ian were on the list.

"I'm not a nut," whispered Matthew to Ian with some indignity in his voice. "Neither am I," replied Ian.

But Ned had now finished with the previous boy and was waiting for the next customer, Matthew, and he had overheard part of their conversation.

"You're both Nuts," said Ned, "hurry up before I hav' t' send for some nutcrackers!"

This was Ned's attempt at humour. It was so out of character and the boys weren't that bright that they could cope with sarcasm, that it meant nothing to them except that Ned thought that they were mentally impaired in some way.

The boys sorted out their free meal tickets and returned to the class.

"Mr. Walkcr says wc'rc nuts," shoutcd Ian as hc camc through thc door. "Hey, Ned's got it right, for once," shouted Gary Dunn from the back of the class.

"OK, OK, that's enough," I said, "sit down you two, let's get back to the Maths."

The class moaned but surprisingly soon settled down except for Matthew and Ian who continued a whispered conversation.

"I'm tellin' me mam," said Ian, "they can't have a notice up that says I'm a nut, it's not right, it's not allowed."

"Me dad'll come down an' sort it out," replied Matthew.

" Hey, you two, let's have a bit less talk and a bit more effort on the sums," I said.

I thought no more about the incident. It was just one of the many silly conversations that teacher's overhear between children, or so I thought.

Peter Milburn was absent for most of the week. So on Wednesday morning I found myself once again on cover with 3C Maths. Things weren't going too badly until the silence of the corridor was broken by two people walking along its bare wooden boards. They went past my classroom towards the staffroom. One was a tall thin man in his early thirties and the other a big woman about twenty years older than the man.

"It's me dad and me grandma," shouted Ian.

We could hear someone knock on the staffroom door and ask to speak to Mr. Walker. Sarah Browne was also free during that lesson and was busy marking some artwork that she'd left in the staffroom. She answered the door. As usual Ned was nowhere to be found so Sarah went off to find Arthur, leaving the couple in the corridor. A few minutes later Arthur arrived covered in sawdust and wood shavings, his glasses still perched on his forehead. "Good morning," said Arthur, "what can I do for you?"

"It's about our Ian being a nut," said the woman, "and he's not a nut. He might be a bit slow like his dad - she pointed to the man - but he's not a nut." "Oh," said Arthur not having a clue what the woman was talking about, "I'm quite sure that he's not a 'nut'."

"Mr. Walker shouldn't have said that," the woman went on, "its not right, I'm not havin' it!"

The woman was now beginning to become annoyed but she didn't realise that she had said the key words that Arthur instinctively knew meant there was likely to be a misunderstanding - Mr. Walker! Arthur intervened,

"Why don't you both come along to my office for a few minutes while we sort it out?"

He ushered the two visitors away from the staffroom and along the corridor towards the upstairs office. He could be heard reassuring the woman,

"I'm sure that it's just a misunderstanding, a mistake. We'll soon have it sorted out."

Throughout the incident the man said nothing.

About ten minutes later the sound of someone coming down the staircase echoed along the silent corridor. The classrooms seemed to become even quieter as everyone strained to here what was being said. There was almost a gasp as the footsteps stopped outside my classroom door. A short knock on the door and it opened as Arthur's head poked through his glasses now in their correct position.

"I'll just have a quick word with young Ian Simpson, if you don't mind."

Ian was out of his seat and half way to the door before I could respond.

Everyone pretended to be working as they listened to the conversation in the corridor.

"What's all this nuts rubbish about?" said Arthur to Ian.

"Mr. Walker said we were nuts," said Ian, "and it was on a list on the wall." Arthur was probably thinking that it sounded just like the sort of comment that Ned would make but asked about the list,

"Show me the list, son."

"It's in the staffroom," said Ian.

They all moved down the corridor and went into the staffroom leaving the door open behind them. It was now so quiet in school that you could have heard a pin drop as everyone desperately tried to hear what was being said.

Ian must have pointed to the list of names on the NUT board.

"You're not nuts, son," sighed Arthur, "you're not even a member."

The man and the boy said nothing just looked vacant. The woman looked puzzled.

"It's the NUT notice board," said Arthur, "the National Union of Teachers, someone's put the list in the wrong place."

"So, no one's saying our Ian's a nut?" asked the woman.

"I'm very sorry," Arthur replied, "its all been a silly mistake. No one's calling Ian. In fact you'll be getting a letter soon telling you about a special class that we're setting up, that Ian will be put into. They'll be called 3S, three special." "D'yer hear that, son," said the woman looking at Ian, "you'll be in a special class."

She smiled and looked contented.

" Thank you, Mr Paterson," she said as she turned to leave the staffroom. She looked up at the man who'd said nothing, the man Ian had called his father,

"Our Ian, special, in a special class. Thank God he's not like you George!"

Truancy has always been a problem in schools, particularly schools like Alton Grange. Many children could see little or no point in school unable to look beyond their present situation and without any ambition. To them school was just something that had to be endured or if you played truant and could get away with it, one bit of suffering that you had avoided. Like many schools Alton Grange had its regular truants. One such boy was William Campbell, who had been an habitual truant throughout his primary school years and now in the second year of his secondary schooling the situation had not improved. He showed all the signs of remaining a member of that group of children for whom school remains a mystery.

Billy was tall for his age but his most remarkable feature was the permanently miserable expression on his face: a face that said, "Why am I here? I hate this place!" To make matters worse if Billy was asked a question his response was always negative and invariably included the words, 'I hate it here'. Billy's record of truancy was one of the worst I've ever seen and despite efforts to encourage Billy to attend school nothing seemed to be working.

After several weeks of absence, Billy returned to school after his parents had been threatened with court proceedings unless his attendance improved. Billy's father brought the boy into the classroom. Mr. Campbell had an even more miserable expression on his face. He looked as if he was carrying all of the world's problems on his shoulders.

"You stop here or I'll end up inside," Mr. Campbell said to his son as he closed the door behind him. There had been no explanation or apology for the interruption; the child had simply been dumped – problem solved!

Of course being away from school for such a long time meant that Billy was way behind the rest of the class. His basic skills in reading and writing were very poor which in itself added fuel to the cycle of truancy, absence and further failings in his education. However, on this occasion he had managed to attend school for a little over two weeks and looked as if he was beginning to settle down, despite a lot of arguments with other children, until we arrived at assembly on Thursday of the third week. On Thursday morning's Billy's class went directly to the top school after assembly for music with Arthur

Johnson. Mr. Johnson taught Maths and music and had a reputation amongst the children as a real tyrant, and to be truthful there was some justification for that label. Billy hated the music lessons. I don't know whether it was actually the music or the teacher or both that he detested but he certainly wasn't keen to be there. So Thursday mornings were always going to be a problem.

Part of the way through the lesson Arthur asked Billy a question about the notes that formed the lines of the treble clef. Billy didn't answer, just looked vacant. Arthur rephrased his question in typical teacher style and asked again.

"How do we remember the names of the notes on the lines?"

Almost all of the other children had raised their hands to answer. This was one of those facts that Arthur had hammered home with his " Every Good Boy Deserves Flogging" routine.

"You see," said Arthur moving across the room to stand directly in front of Billy and bending down to eye level while the whole class listened intently, "if you were here a bit more often you'd have known the answer to that one. You're just like your father was. He was never here. He wouldn't have known the answer either."

Billy looked as if he was going to reply but he must have had second thoughts or been able to sense that it wouldn't be a good idea, so he kept his mouth shut. Billy was fortunate really because Arthur left it at that. He must have been in a good mood because he was renowned for his bad temper.

That afternoon at registration Billy was missing again. It was the same story the following morning and the boy who had been told to call for Billy each day as part of the return to school regime said that Billy had told him that he was not going to school anymore. School was left with no option this time and a procedure had to be put into action because of the previous serious truancies.

Arthur contacted Jean the secretary at the top school who tried to telephone the home at various times in the day but without success. A standard letter was put in the post to meet the school's responsibilities but there was no response. Then one Thursday afternoon there was a phone call asking specifically for Mr. Paterson, the deputy head. I had heard the telephone ringing in the upstairs office and as my classroom was close by I was expected to answer those calls, taking messages if necessary because Arthur taught a full timetable and couldn't always just leave everything. However, on this occasion the voice on the phone was most insistent that they speak directly to Arthur so I felt obliged to go and find him.

The person on the telephone said,

"It's about our Billy."

"Billy who?" asked Arthur.

"Our Billy, Billy Campbell," said the voice, "he's been proper bad, really bad, so don't bother t' send the kiddy catcher around, will you?"

Arthur was listening very carefully to the voice, which seemed a bit anxious and rather young, making him somewhat suspicious.

"I'm sorry," he said down the mouth piece of the telephone, "the system's all set up and happens automatically. Billy's been off so often someone's bound to come out."

"No, no, you can't do that, "came the reply even more anxious and rather high pitched, clearly becoming agitated.

"Who's speaking?" snapped Arthur sharply.

"It's me dad," said the voice.

There was a short pause, then realising his mistake the line went dead. Billy must have put down the receiver. I had overheard most of the conversation on my way out of the room.

"It's me dad," said Arthur, a smile on his face. "I'd better ask Jean to send the welfare officer around to the Campbell's."

I was always surprised by the huge range of ability in my classes, especially since they were supposed to have been arranged in ability sets. 1A was no exception and it was not until quite late in the year that I began to realise that sometimes the setting was nothing to do with academic ability, more a question of behaviour or learning difficulty. On the whole 1A were probably my best class during that first year. I suppose that we were both new to the school and they were still keen to learn without all the prejudices that older children quickly acquire. Most of them were happy pleasant children who seemed to like their Maths lessons. However, there were one or two children who found Maths to be a complete mystery, sometimes because of their primary school experiences but occasionally for other reasons. Jack Hardy was one such boy. He had been run down by a bus one day on his way home from primary school and suffered head injuries. Although he had made a full recovery and was considered fit for mainstream school he had a number of fairly severe learning difficulties and tended to take everything quite literally.

We were doing an exercise on linear measurement and as it was a warm, sunny day I thought that I would take the class outside to measure a range of objects such as the length of the school yard, a brick in the wall, the distance between lines drawn on the playground and so on. I wouldn't have dared to risk that much freedom with most of my classes but I felt that I had built a good relationship with 1A and should give it a try. I explained to the class how we were going to make the measurements, the equipment that they were to use etc. but said that before they went outside there were some inside measurements to take. One was to measure the length of their desk amongst other things. Most children quickly dealt with the internal measurements recording them in their exercise books as requested, then moved out into the playground to complete the task. But Jack was having great difficulty measuring his desk. I went across to him and asked if I could help,

"What's the problem, Jack?" I asked.

"This ruler's not long enough," replied Jack in a low gruff voice.

"So what do you think we should do?" I asked.

The boy thought for a minute, then said,

"I've tried stretching it, but it won't and you said use the ruler to measure your desk."

I hadn't thought it would be necessary to explain what to do if the object being measured was longer than the ruler.

Outside, one of the girls, Elizabeth Turner, was having problems measuring the yard, mainly because Jeff Gray who had been "free" and seen what was going on through the staffroom annex window had decided to 'help'. Jeff stopped Elizabeth part of the way across the yard as she counted the number of times she had used her metre rule.

"What're you up to?" asked Jeff.

But before she could answer he'd asked another question,

"What's the date today? What's the date of your birthday? How many people are there in your class? How old are you?"

And so it went on. Lots of questions all with numerical answers and Elizabeth doing her best to answer them. Then Jeff said,

"Anyway, sorry to stop you. You'll be wanting to get on."

The girl looked a bit puzzled then her face changed to a frown as she realised that she'd forgotten how many turns of the metre rule she had made. Jeff started to smile.

"Oh, sir, you did that deliberately," she said to Jeff.

"Who me?" said Jeff a wry smile on his face.

The girl walked back to the end of the wall and started to measure again. Jeff looked at me as I stood on the steps near the entrance watching what was going on.

"Just thought I'd lend a hand," he shouted across the yard.

"I'm sure that you'll be a 'big help'," I replied.

11

COMMUTING.

Split site schools were fairly common during the 1970's in Durham as well as many other parts of the country. Often they were the result of school mergers, or single sex schools joining to form one coeducational establishment or occasionally as a result of falling roles. At Alton Grange the merger of the separate Boys and Girls Schools' had taken place some years earlier and had been compounded by falling numbers with the closure of the colliery and the movement of families seeking other sources of employment. The two buildings were about half a mile apart. However, the premises were not really suitable as there was not a complete duplication of facilities and the lower school building was very old and in a poor state of repair. There had been talk of school closure for at least the previous ten years and the consensus was that this was the reason for the neglected state of the lower school building. That talk of closure continued throughout my time at Alton Grange.

The Local Authority's solution to a lack of duplication of facilities was to commute staff or children or both from one site to the other as the needs of the timetable demanded. The idea was to minimise the movement by working on one site for all of one day or at least all of one half-day session. In practice this wasn't always feasible and children were sometimes commuted between sites mid session. The teaching time lost must have been a real problem for the authorities but for the staff it was often a real Godsend, particularly if you had a difficult class, which in those early days seemed to be most of them.

The actual process of commuting left itself wide open to abuse by both staff and pupils. Staff with difficult classes often left the school early and dawdled along the Main Street. This would at least get the children out of the classroom and gave the teacher some respite. However, once the children were out of the constraints of the classroom, they could be much worse to control. A typical example of the trials of commuting took place one Tuesday afternoon when I was due to commute 2B up to the top school for music and exchange at the half way point with Andy Jackson who was bringing 3C down to the bottom school for art. It was about two o'clock and I was wondering how I was going to keep 2B's interest in "White Fang" for another twenty minutes until it was time to commute when a girl appeared at the classroom door. She knocked and came into the room carrying a folded piece of paper. It was a note from Jeff. I opened it and read,

"Bet yours are driving you round the bend just like mine. I can't stand anymore of them so I'm commuting at ten past even if its tipping it down!"

The normal practice was to decide at about ten past two if the weather was reasonable enough to commute. This really meant that if it was pouring with rain you stayed put, giving you another twenty minutes of purgatory and the prospect of a different class next lesson, not the one on the timetable because they wouldn't have commuted either. So as far as possible staff always tried to commute. Unfortunately there was rarely any communication between sites so if you left a little early your counterpart on the other site might not leave if the weather was at all suspect leaving you with no one to swap classes with at the halfway stage.

As soon as it reached ten past two we could hear the clatter of chairs being moved on the wooden floors of Jeff's classroom and the noise of children moving into the corridor. 2B immediately took this to mean that it was time to commute. The reading stopped and the shuffling of books began as the children packed away their belongings.

"Just a minute," I called looking over my book at the class, "we're not going anywhere just yet, Gail's not finished."

Gail had been reading a paragraph of the reader out loud to the rest of the class. This was standard practice at that time to improve children's reading skills and build their confidence to speak in public. I doubt whether the experts had considered the problems of adolescent embarrassment, awkwardness and low self-esteem. "Get them to read out loud, as often as you can," the head of English had told me at the beginning of that term. He hadn't told me how difficult it could be.

Gail finished the sentence and sat down. I could see how restless things were becoming so I said nothing just closed the book. This was the signal that they were waiting for and a frenzy of bag packing, getting coats on, stealing each other's pencil cases and so on broke out. A minute or two later we were ready for the off. Just as I opened the classroom door Arthur was coming along the corridor from the office.

"Bit early aren't you?" he said looking at his watch.

"Eh, Jeff's already gone," I said, "I thought we were late."

Arthur said nothing but looked disappointed. I immediately felt guilty, that I had let him down and I decided that I wouldn't do this again, but with 2B pushing past me as they stampeded out of the door, the decision had already been made on this occasion.

People usually think of groups of children out of the classroom walking along in neat quiet crocodiles, the pairs talking sensibly as they keep together with the teacher walking behind their proud brood. Commuting with 2B wasn't much like that! The idea was to try to keep together as a class; no one getting too far ahead and no one dragging behind. They were told not to block the street or walk in the way of members of the public. They knew that they had to stop at strategic points such as the bottom school gates to cross the main street, the pedestrian crossing and the junction opposite the Co-op. In reality it wasn't the neat crocodile described previously, it was more like a walk with "the Bash Street Kids" of Beano fame and a crocodile might have come in handy to keep them in order.

As usual 2B were all over the place. They could see Jeff's class ahead of them. I was trying to shepherd them towards a safe spot to cross the main street, which seemed to be busier than usual. I wasn't into standing in the middle of the road stopping the traffic, as some staff seemed to like to do. With this motley crew the traffic would have probably kept going. Instead I was watching for a gap in the traffic and we could then make a dash for it. As I looked along the road the class seemed to be smaller. I started counting them as best I could, then I noticed Graham and Ian come out of the butcher's shop each eating a large bread bun filled with some sort of meat. Joe Dawson was coming out of Thubron's newsagents lighting a cigarette as he walked along the street.

"Put that out," I shouted.

"By, you've got your hands full," said an old man standing at the roadside close to where we were trying to cross. He was holding a bicycle with a bag of coal across its crossbar.

"I wouldn't have your job for all the tea in China," he went on.

I smiled politely and hurried after the class who were now all across the road and tearing down the main street after Jeff's class.

Some of the children had by now reached the pedestrian crossing and were playing "dare" with the traffic by putting one foot out onto the first road marking of the crossing as a vehicle approached, then stepping back off the crossing as the vehicle stopped.

"Stop messing about!" I shouted as I arrived at the crossing, a large petrol tanker having just squealed to a halt trying to avoid knocking down Tracey Bowman, one of the "dare the traffic" brigade.

"Just get across the road, before this driver gets anymore annoyed."

The children moved out onto the crossing and over the road. I mouthed thank you to the driver who shook his head in sympathy with my situation. Commuting was one of those occasions when you were on view to the public, whose expectations of good behaviour and courtesy from the children were very high. I always felt that I couldn't reach their standards with 2B. People would stand to one side, not just to avoid being trampled but also to watch how the teacher controlled the group or in this case failed to control the group. Many of them were probably like the old man with the bicycle – just thankful that it wasn't their problem, but I always felt on trial.

We managed to complete the road crossing despite Brian climbing up the beacon at the other side of the road, and made our way towards the junction opposite to the Co-op.

"I'm just going to see me mam in the Co-op," shouted Sharon, a girl from 2B as she disappeared into the shop.

I couldn't have stopped her if I'd tried. We hurried across the road and started the climb up to the top school. This was always the slowest part of the journey and an opportunity to try to regain some semblance of control before the change over of classes. But this time all of the children stopped outside one of the houses. It was the home of another member of 2B, Walter Atkinson, bother of Jacqueline who had told me that her brother was off school because he was ill –

" Proper bad, sir, he couldn't get up this mornin'."

Walter was digging a trench in the garden.

"I thought you were ill, Walter?" I asked as I approached the garden.

"I'm better now, but me dad wants 'us to dig this leek trench or else," replied the boy.

Just then the door of the house opened and a big man appeared. He was wearing trousers and a vest with his trouser braces over one shoulder. He wasn't wearing shoes and was carrying a newspaper in front of him as though he was reading it. He saw the crowd of children with me as I stood towards the back of the group.

"What's he want, our Walter?" said the man beckoning towards me with his eyes.

"Oh, he's just blethering on about summut," replied the boy.

"Take nee notice son, get that trench dug, mind," said the man ignoring me completely as he slammed shut the door, the broken pane of glass in its upper half rattling ready to fall.

"I've got your report on my desk," I said to Walter trying to move on, "I could ask your sister to bring it home for you."

"No, no, just hoy it in the back o' the cree as you gan' back down t'the bottom school," replied the boy turning his back on me and the children jeering over the fence.

Just then Bill Edwards appeared at the top of the hill with 3C my change over group. Bill had them in a much more orderly manner and had already stopped the first of 2B making them line up properly.

" By, you must have had an early start," he said, "or are we late?"

"I think we're both about on time," I said unconvincingly, "its just 2B can't wait to get to technical drawing and needlework."

Bill beamed, he liked the idea that the children were keen to get to his class when in fact most of them hated it.

We exchanged classes and as Bill walked off with 2B, 3C broke into a shambles. The orderly group of children had now descended into a run away rabble with children everywhere. I was very concerned about it but no one else seemed worried at all. I realised years later that it took months if not years to build any sort of relationship with groups like 3C let alone to be able to control them outside of the classroom situation.

We walked back to the bottom school and the children vanished into the playground amongst the other children having their afternoon break. The group that you commuted were not always the group that you were going to teach. Thankfully on this occasion I had 1A for Maths and 3C were going to Margaret for Geography. Break came to an end and the children came in for their next lesson.

I had just started another riveting lesson on ratio with 1A when Margaret appeared at the door.

"Could I have a word?" she asked as she opened the door.

I went to the door.

"Did you bring 3C down from the top school?" she asked, "because I've only got four of them in my room."

"Yes, they were messing about a bit and all other the place, but I think most of them were there," I said sheepishly, "I wonder where they've gone?"

" No problem," said Margaret, "sorry to have bothered you, as long as they're not trying to mess me about, the fewer the better."

With that she closed the door and set off back to her class. I wasn't really sure what to do but as always in teaching there's no time to think because there's always a class waiting and my priority turned back to 1A.

The following day the mystery was solved. On our commute the previous afternoon we had seen Ned's brown Ford Escort chugging down the hill, obviously not running properly. He hadn't acknowledged us, waved or anything but that was quite normal for Ned. It seems that his car had broken down just as he was coming through the gates to the bottom school. He had enlisted the help of 3C to push the car into the school yard and some of the engineering experts in 3C had offered to "fix it for yer, sir." Ned had opened the bonnet and was having a cigarette as the boys looked vaguely at the engine. He hadn't thought to let Margaret know that most of her class was 'helping him'.

So a typical commute was always a bit of a trauma and another opportunity to 'blether on' at the children. However, the fact that children were used to walking between the two sites meant that both the public and other children didn't question why children were not in lessons and could be out and about on the streets. This situation was open to abuse by staff but could be useful as a cooling off period when dealing with a difficult child. Some staff occasionally would send such children to the other site on the pretext of delivering a message or taking some books or equipment to the other site. This gave both the child and the member of staff that vital few minutes to cool off before continuing with the lesson. Everyone knew that it went on and no one seemed unnecessarily worried about it, unlike the Health and Safety concerns that would be raised today, let alone the loss of teaching time, and it did provide a way of avoiding problems or allowing a minor difficulty to escalate. Unfortunately it could be misused.

George Raine was having a difficult time trying to explain some of the physics of simple machines to a reluctant 3B. He was demonstrating pulleys using some of the class to participate but things were not going very smoothly. George had been a pupil at the school many years previously. He had left school and trained as an electrical engineer at the local colliery before deciding to move into teaching. He had been a victim of the practical jokes often played on apprentices and thought that he would use one of them to have a breather from one of the nuisances in his class who was not paying attention.

"Oh, that's the problem," said George to the class of children sat around the teacher's demonstration bench, "no wonder it won't work."

"Why's that?" asked Trevor Foreman, one of the few boys in the class who was paying attention.

"We need a sky hook to secure the top pulley," replied George.

"What's a sky hook?" asked Trevor.

"Well its, er, um, perhaps Mr. Gray could send one down from the top school. I'll just give him a ring or perhaps someone could run up and collect it."

The thought of getting out of science to stroll slowly up to the top school then dawdle back down to the bottom school was enough for a sea of volunteering hands all yelling, "me sir, send me."

George looked around the room at the motley crew, his eyes fixing on Darren Butts busily carving something into the bench with a short knife.

"Ah good, Darren could go," said George.

"Oh, that's not fair, can't I go?" moaned most of the class.

George ignored the moaning.

"Right, Darren," he said, "run up to the top school and ask Mr. Gray for a sky hook. He'll know what you mean."

"Do I have to?" asked Darren.

"Just go and ask, hurry up," replied George ignoring the protestations. Reluctantly the boy left the class.

It was about twenty minutes later when the boy returned, empty-handed. "Where's the sky hook?" asked George.

"You didn't tell me what size," replied Darren, "Mr. Gray said that he needed to know the size."

"I'm sorry lad," said George, "Nip back up and tell him that a six inch triple will do. You'll have time before the end of the lesson if you run."

The boy started to protest again but noticed that the rest of the class were busy doing some calculations on pulleys, so suddenly stopped talking and left to do the errand. Another fifteen minutes passed and the now red-faced Darren appeared at the door again, once more empty-handed.

"Are you alright, lad," said George, "you look a bit out of breath. Have you got the sky hook?"

" I've just been chased by that big black Alsatian at the Corner House. It jumped over the fence and I thought it was going to bite me. And I'd only been poking it with a stick through the fence."

" Sky hook?" asked George.

The boy looked even more vacant than usual, then seemed to remember as he screwed up his face while he concentrated to remember the message,

"Mr Gray says he hasn't got any triples but will a double do?"

" Oh, that'll be fine," said George, "did you bring one?"

" Well no," replied Darren, "I didn't know whether it would be any good."

"Look," said George, "I know that the bell's about to go but because you now know all about sky hooks, could you just pop back up to the top school and tell Mr. Gray that a double will be fine. Don't worry about your next lesson I'll sort that out. Who do you have next?"

"Mrs. Jackson," replied Darren, "but do I have to go?"

"Course you do," said George, "Mrs. Jackson won't mind and you are the sky hooks expert."

"But that dog'll be after me," protested Darren.

"No, it'll be gone by now. Anyway you could round by the chapel," suggested George, "go on, off you go."

The sky hook saga went on for most of the day with Darren walking between sites. No one complained and in fact most staff that would have been teaching him were pleased that he wasn't present. There were questions about the colour of the sky hook, the number of mounting holes that it needed to have, whether it was left handed or right handed and so on. Darren got more and more frustrated but didn't once question the existence of the sky hook. What's even more surprising was that no one else in the class questioned it either. They all seemed to believe that it was a bona fide piece of apparatus.

By late afternoon Darren was still trotting from site to site. I think George took pity on him and felt a little guilty when he told the boy that the sky hook didn't exist and tried to explain to him that it was a practical joke of the sort that might well be played on him when he started work. George tried to warn Darren about long stands, pails full of nail holes and the like but I'm not sure that Darren really understood because he wasn't annoyed he just said,

"So there's not really a suitable sky hook, so how will you fix up the experiment?"

12

PASSING THE BUCK.

As the summer term approached I felt a little more settled, perhaps resigned to my chosen career which was turning out to be nothing like I had imagined or been led to believe. The reality was much more difficult than the theory. I was beginning to learn some of the basics of survival in this most demanding of jobs: the tricks of the trade having realised that college had been no preparation at all and that my own experiences of school were far from the norm and certainly totally different from my current experience. I was beginning to have a much clearer view of how things worked in school. Some might say a cynical view but I always considered myself to be realistic rather than cynical.

However, I never failed to be amazed by Ned's ability to 'pass the buck'. He was able to avoid issues, work, particularly important things and especially anything concerning the children with skills that would parallel the best professional football player. This is not to say that he did not care, more that he didn't want to be involved if the issue might have any direct impact on him.

Without fail the problem would fall back onto the shoulders of the deputy head, Arthur Paterson, who would deal with it while Ned took the praise. How often I was to see this scenario repeated over the next thirty years: people in senior positions unable to cope themselves and only too keen to pass on the responsibility under the guise of delegation. I'm sure that it happens in all walks of life, but in this instance it was so glaringly obvious with no attempt to disguise the truth. Two incidents in particular, from the dozens that occurred during that first year highlighted Ned's ability to side step a problem and let Arthur deal with it.

The first took place one Wednesday morning in mid May. Looking back something must have been going on earlier in the week or perhaps for several weeks but no one either took any notice or particularly cared. It was morning break and unusually Simon Bateson was in the staffroom pouring tea as I walked in.

"Alright, lad," he said, "tea? How'yer getting on?"

"OK, I think," I replied, not really very sure what to say.

Simon was a PE teacher who usually worked at the upper school but had been told to come down to the lower school to cover a staff absence. More staff began entering the staffroom and Simon's attention was drawn to them. "I've got 2C for English for Sarah Browne. Anybody got any ideas what I can do with them?" asked Simon.

"Well you could read them a story," smirked Brian Chapman, "they like a good story, puts them to sleep."

"Alright, OK, we all remember the last time I followed your bright idea. I'm never going to live that down, am I?" replied Simon. "No, I need something that they can get on with while I fill in me Pools coupon. It's got to be my turn with Littlewood's. Any ideas?" said Simon trying again.

"Most of them can't write much," started Margaret.

"No, you mean, most of them can't write anything," interrupted Brian.

"I would read them a short story or a poem and ask them to draw a picture to describe what it means to them," continued Margaret.

"That'll never keep them going all lesson," said Simon.

"Yes, it will if you tell them to colour it in as well and offer a prize for the best one," said Margaret, "I've done it myself when we've been looking at a new city in geography."

"It's got to be worth a Mars bar, at least," said Brian, "send somebody to Albert's before the end of break."

"Do you really think so?" asked Simon looking directly at Margaret.

She nodded as she drank her tea.

"OK then, I'll give it a try, but you'll have to lend me some money Brian, mine's at the top school" said Simon.

"Bloody typical," retorted Brian, "and I want it back, mind."

He handed some money to Simon who walked to the window of the staffroom annex and beckoned to some girls who were standing by the boiler house door. As soon as they saw that it was Simon, there was a mad rush towards the window. Simon was using his heart throb image to the full. He opened the window and asked one of the girls to go to the ice cream parlour next door for the 'prize'. As he closed the window he turned to Brian and said, "By the way, have you seen the state of that bottom field. It looks as though its sinking."

Brian also taught some PE and knew what Simon was talking about. The rest of us sat eavesdropping not really understanding much of the conversation as we drank our tea.

"Sinking?" replied Brian, "you must have had too many last night."

They left it at that as the bell rang and we went off to our classes. Arthur was just on his way to the staffroom having answered a telephone call from Ned who had a habit of ringing at break. He didn't make it into the staffroom that break, so he wasn't aware of the conversation, as he turned to stand in the corridor looking menacingly at the children as they filed into their classes in silence.

On Friday morning there was a noticeable buzz amongst the children as they came into registration. They were all eager to tell me something.

"Just a minute," I said, "sit down and we'll do the register first, then you can tell me the news."

"But it's important," shouted out Jacqueline Atkinson in her usual forthright manner, "the top school's going to fall into a big hole."

" Fall into a hole? What d'you mean?" I asked.

"The goal post's have already gone," shouted Sean Tindle from the back of the class.

After several more similar comments I eventually discovered that a large hole had appeared overnight on one of the playing fields on the upper school site. It was probably a landfall resulting from some underground mine workings or settlement since the colliery's closure. The whole area was known to be a warren of mine workings going back into history.

"Can we go and see it?" asked Sharon Giles.

"No, no," I said, "it's just a hole. You'd best all keep away from it in case you fall in."

"Where would you go if you did fall in?" asked Sharon.

"Look, never mind all that, just keep away from it," I said.

Just then the bell rang and I sent the class out to their first lesson.

At break the hole in the playing field was the main topic of conversation in the staffroom, particularly questions about what was going to happen. We were just as curious as the children. Then the door burst open and in stormed Ned in his usual harassed state,

"Where's Paterson?" he yelled, "never bloody here when you need him!" This was most unfair because Arthur carried Ned through all sorts of problems as I mentioned earlier. Ned took off his wet coat and shook it in front of the open coal fire. The rain from the coat hitting the hot embers of the fire hissed and spewed out belches of thick black smoke.

"Ned, will you be careful. I'm getting soaked here," complained Margaret who was sitting in her usual chair close to the fire drinking a cup of tea. Ned was oblivious of his actions and said nothing.

Arthur appeared at the window in the door, saw Ned and the expression on his face changed from a smile to that questioning look that wonders what is about to happen.

"Ah, good Arthur," said Ned, "I've got to go t' County Hall and there's been some bother on a field at the top school. So I'll just finish this tea and I'll be away. You can sort that field business out, right."

"Well Ned, I'm teaching, you know," replied Arthur but Ned wasn't listening as usual.

"That's champion," said Ned, "I'll be off then."

With that he threw the tea leaves from his cup into the open coal fire creating another cloud of smoke and more protestations from Margaret and off he shot out of the building.

Arthur stood shaking his head. He didn't want to be disloyal but he said, "He's a bugger, Ned, he knows I've classes to teach and things to sort out. I suppose I'll have to sort out this problem at the top school. Anyone know what's been going on?"

But before we could answer Arthur was already looking at the timetable trying to organise some cover for his classes. The rest of the staff continued to discuss the hole and Ned's actions.

Later that day we found out that Arthur had dealt with the problem in his normal matter of fact way. He had arranged for the area to be isolated and on the advice of the Local Authority he had contacted the NCB who were sending an engineer out to assess the situation. So, in fact the problem had been easily addressed: things that Ned could easily have done himself. We all suspected that there was no meeting at County Hall but of course we were unable to find out.

A few days later lorries started to arrive at the upper school with a huge quantity of rubble which they tipped into the hole. Eventually it was capped with concrete before a new covering of soil was laid. Ned's only comment about the incident came one lunchtime the following week, when he had called into the lower school to tell Arthur that someone was coming from County Hall and he would be out at the Parish Council meeting.

"Here, Arthur by the way, you know that hole that I had filled in, the one in the field at the top school," said Ned, "the buggers never took the goal posts out first."

Arthur looked in amazement at the comments and his face changed. He started to speak sounding like Sooty's right hand man, Harry Corbett,

"I'll sort it out Ned, supposing that I have to make new goal posts myself."

Another example of Ned's 'buck passing prowess' happened a few weeks later and could have had much more serious consequences.

Children often brought things into school to show their friends or sometimes to show the teacher: new toys, books, things that they'd been given for their birthday and that type of thing. I thought that it was important to take an interest so they often included me in their new treasures. So it wasn't anything out of the ordinary when William and Barry McQuire said that they'd brought in something that they'd dug up in the garden and to be truthful I wasn't really listening as it was registration and there were a lot of other things going on. I thought that it was probably some old coins or a dog's bone so I was rather surprised when they pulled out a large metal cylinder wrapped in a piece of old sacking. As they removed the sacking, the familiar dark green colouring and shape of a shell, probably from World War 11, became apparent.

"Did someone bring it back from the War then, a souvenir?" I asked.

"No," said Barry, "we dug it up last night in our dad's garden."

I paused for a moment and thought. It couldn't be an unexploded shell, no it would be a training item or something similar. Still it would be wise to take no chances so I'd better send for Arthur. He arrived a few minutes later looking surprised by the shell on the desk.

"Souvenir, eh?" he said as he came across the room.

But then the look on his face changed as he noticed something that meant far more to him than the rest of us. He remained totally calm but said,

"I think we'd better move these children away from this. Take them to the hall. At once please."

I did as requested and waited to find out what was going on only to be pestered by Barry asking,

"Can we have our bomb back please?"

Arthur said that he was pretty sure that it was an incendiary bomb but he suspected that a rusted detonator might still be present in the side of the casing and although it looked harmless it might still be live.

"I'd better let Ned know, I suppose," he said as he left the room, "keep this room locked and I'm afraid you'll have to work in the hall for the moment."

I expected Ned to appear soon after Arthur's telephone call but there was no response. About half past eleven the clatter of Ned's familiar gait could be heard in the corridor and the smell of cigarettes drifted into the classrooms but still nothing happened. The bell rang for the end of the morning session. The children went off for lunch and the staff headed for the staffroom as usual expecting Ned to tell us what he was going to do.

Ned was sat at the table waiting for his lunch as Arthur came into the room. "That shell, Ned, what's happening?" asked Arthur.

"Oh, bloody Hell," snapped Ned, "D'yer think I've nowt else to do. I'm up to me neck in it. Get onto the people from County about it, Arthur. I'm away home for me dinner!"

With that Ned sprang to his feet, picked up his coat and vanished through the staffroom door. We all looked at each other not knowing whether to laugh or what to say. But the expression on Arthur's face said it all – sheer disbelief.

"I'd better ring them straight away," sighed Arthur, "it's still in your classroom, Michael, isn't it?"

"Yes, I locked it in there and we've worked in the hall this morning," I said. But the conversation was interrupted by Brian Chapman.

"Bomb, did you say? A real bomb? Oh Hell! Young Barry McQuire was pestering me to get something from your room," said Brian gesturing towards me, "so I gave him my keys. I didn't really take much notice of what he said. He wouldn't take it, would he?"

Arthur shook his head in disbelief of what he was hearing.

"I'll go and find out," I said to Arthur.

I jumped up from my seat and hurried to the classroom only to find that as expected Barry had taken the shell. I rushed back to the staffroom and reported back to Arthur.

"God, I wonder where they've gone," said Arthur.

I looked at the large hand written copy of the timetable pinned on the notice board.

"They've got music at the top school first thing this afternoon," I said, "perhaps they've taken it with them?"

"I'll ring the top school," said Arthur, "perhaps we can find them."

About fifteen minutes later the telephone rang, just as we were about to eat dessert – a watery rice pudding with something like a dollop of jam or rose hip syrup in it. George passed the phone to Arthur. It turned out that the two brothers had indeed gone to the top school and were very busy showing off their prize exhibit to other children as Arthur Johnson had found them. He had confiscated the shell and was awaiting instructions. There was no sign of Ned. Arthur (the deputy head) went off to the office. Several telephone calls later he returned to finish his lunch and explain what was going to happen.

"County Hall have advised me to put the shell in the middle of the top playing field, obviously keep all the kids away and they'll inform the bomb squad who they expect will come out to deal with it later this afternoon because they'll have to come from Catterick."

Two o'clock came and nothing had happened so everyone made excuses to commute early in the hope that they might see something. At about half past two a bomb squad vehicle arrived at the top school. Jeff had commuted his class and was then free so he stayed at the top school to see what was going to happen. He later related the story to the rest of the bottom school staff. "One of the army lads had a look at it. He had all the protective gear on, full face mask, body armour and that. He shouted back to the officer that it could be live and was probably an unexploded incendiary device from the War. He didn't sound very sure. They decided that the safest way to disarm it was with a controlled explosion. They surrounded the shell with sandbags and one of the technicians did something to it. I couldn't really see what. Anyway we were too far back and shouldn't really have been there at all. One of the blokes came back unwinding a coil of wire, which he connected to one of those plunger things like you see on the telly. They checked that everyone was out of the way, then sounded a siren and someone shouted 'Stand clear'. The officer pushed the plunger down and an almighty bang went off as the sandbags were blown up into the air."

"We heard the noise down here," said Margaret.

"Once the smoke had cleared," said Jeff, "you could see an almighty big hole in that top field. Ned'll not be very happy about that."

Just then there was a knock at the staffroom door. It was the McQuire brothers.

"Can we have what's left of our bomb?" asked Barry.

"No you bloody well can't," replied Arthur sharply, "anyway there'll not be much left now. Go on, off you go home and don't go digging anymore up in the garden; or if you do, leave them at home."

The following day Ned's car pulled into the bottom school yard just before morning break. As usual the silence of the corridor was broken by Ned striking a match to light his cigarette. He paused outside Arthur's room. Everyone was silent listening in to the conversation.

"I got that shell sorted out, Ned," started Arthur.

"I know," snarled Ned, "it woke me up. I thought I was back on the boats. I was just having forty winks afore I came back to work to sort it."

"You'd been busy then," said Arthur sarcastically.

"Oh, aye. Yer knaw me always full o' graft," replied Ned not listening or realising what Arthur was getting at, his cigarette bobbing up and down in the corner of his mouth as he spoke.

"I'd just been getting' some shoppin' and nipped into the butcher's for some steak. You know I like a bit of T-bone. Oh, bugger it, I forgot the sausages." With that Ned turned and was out of school as quickly as he had come in. There was no mention of school, the events of the afternoon, or any thanks to Arthur for dealing with it.

Over the next few years I was to see Ned repeat this sort of behaviour regularly. Each time Arthur sorted out the problem without any thanks or praise. Ned was always too busy. What's more I was to see other senior managers do the same sort of 'buck passing' many times over the next few years, only now it was called delegation. I expect we've all witnessed it in our own walks of life.

13

INSPECTIONS

OFSTED has become the nightmare of inspection for schools today but inspection is not a new phenomenon. In the early and mid 1970's inspection seemed to occur with just as much frequency but had a much different emphasis, with less direct criticism of teachers and a greater recognition of the problems that they were dealing with on a day to day basis. League tables, raising achievement, dumbing down and so on may well have been going on but to the classroom teacher at the chalk face, survival was the main concern. The football hooligan of Saturday was in your classroom on Monday morning and of course it continues today.

Inspection came in many forms, mostly on a much less formal basis than today often without the need for direct classroom observation followed by a post mortem of the lesson, which all good teachers are only too good at doing anyway! I have no memory of actually being formally observed with a class by the deputy head during that first year but I am sure that he knew what my strengths and weaknesses were and he gave excellent advice and support throughout my time in that school.

More formal inspections came from organisations beyond the school and took the form of Local Authority inspection of probationary teachers or occasionally a brief visit by Her Majesty's Inspectorate of Schools (HMI).

Unusually HMI visited Alton Grange twice in the first year: something to do with "the reorganisation of the educational provision in the area". On each visit the inspectors were men in their late fifties immaculately dressed in dark suits with perfect ties and not a hair out of place wearing exceptionally well polished shoes. In my experience, they were always pleasant, polite people who were keen to talk to the children and involve themselves in the lesson by sitting with the children, raising their hands to answer questions and taking part in the practical work of science lessons. Their feedback contained no hint of criticism and no negative judgements only praise for " an excellent job done in exceptionally difficult circumstances". How things were to change when I reflect on the Gestapo style interrogation of my most recent 'interview' with a member of the current HMI, and he was wearing suede shoes.

As probationary teachers the most traumatic event was the Local Authority inspector's visit that determined whether you could complete your probationary year and obtain full teacher status, giving you freedom from further scrutiny by the Local Authority other than an occasional visit, a bit like passing your driving test. Several of us were in this position and each of us dreaded the day. There was to be no warning. Someone would arrive from County Hall to observe the probationary teacher with one or two classes and make a judgement as to whether you passed or failed. It was not a foregone conclusion that you would pass and indeed some did fail. However, among other qualified young teachers the tormenting of probationers was a source of amusement with tales of how difficult it could be to pass and how awkward the inspectors might be.

This tormenting was highlighted one day in late May when an 'inspector' arrived unannounced to observe Sarah Browne with a second year art class. Sarah had started teaching at Alton Grange at the same time as myself. She was teaching mainly art and had proved herself to be a very competent, if rather formidable teacher. She had been part of a group known as 'mature students'. A lady in her mid forties who had chosen to go into teaching after her own children were settled in their secondary schools. Sarah was firm with the children, didn't seem to like anyone very much and constantly moaned about Ned and his lack of leadership and organisation. She worked most closely with Dennis Black who was senior art teacher and head of department. Dennis was another real character with a great sense of humour. He played the drums in a comedy show band at weekends and some evenings. The idea of an inspection in the art department was just too good an opportunity to miss.

Dennis decided that he would 'inspect' one of Sarah's lessons by disguising himself as the inspector for Sarah's probationary observation. The plan was to sit in on a lesson, make a few outrageous suggestions, then leave having 'passed' Sarah; at least that was the plan.

The second lesson of the day had just started when Dennis put his plan into action. Instead of his usual jeans and T- shirt, he was dressed in a dark suit with a bowler hat and carrying an umbrella. He was wearing spectacles and a false moustache and had produced a fairly convincing disguise. It was not easy to tell that it was Dennis and if you weren't expecting him I doubt whether you would have been able to tell. Sarah had no idea of what was going on, unlike the rest of the staff and many of the children, except for Sarah's class from whom it had been kept a closely guarded secret. She was aware that sometime in the near future someone would be coming out from the Local Authority to see her.

Arthur looked at Dennis in his disguise, shook his head, smiled but said nothing. Dennis sent a boy from his class, sworn to secrecy, down to Sarah's classroom to tell her that an inspector had arrived from County Hall and was on his way to see her. A few minutes later Dennis set off for the classroom. As he approached the classroom he could see through the windows in the corridor that Sarah was busy explaining to the class what they were going to do. As Dennis passed almost all of the children's eyes turned away from Sarah and onto the figure in the corridor. Dennis knocked on the door and Sarah asked him in barely stopping her explanation and clearly a bit flustered. Dennis said nothing knowing that as soon as he spoke Sarah might recognise his voice. Sarah assumed that he was the inspector. Dennis gestured to continue the lesson, smiled and sat down at the back of the room. Most of the children turned their attention back to Sarah, ignoring Dennis and probably just thinking he was another visitor, except for two small boys sitting just opposite to Dennis who continued to stare at the 'inspector'.

After a few minutes one of the boys began to smile, realising who the 'inspector' actually was. He whispered something to his friend sitting next to him, who then starred at Dennis, who in turn tried to encourage the boys to look away and become involved in the lesson. Then the second boy put up his hand.

"What is it, Daniel?" asked Sarah wondering why the boy could be asking a question at that particular point and obviously a little more anxious than usual wondering what the inspector would make of it.

"Mrs Browne," said Daniel, "why's Mr Black sat here wearing a bowler hat? Is it a new game?"

The whole class turned and looked closely at Dennis then started to laugh. Dennis stood up took off the Bowler hat, which he had forgotten to remove as he came in, smiled and started to laugh. But Sarah was far from laughter. She was clearly furious and not in the least amused. Dennis took one look at her, said nothing and left the classroom in a hurry.

News of the event spread like wildfire around the school but it was weeks before Sarah forgave Dennis.

Probationary inspections always seemed to happen when they were least expected and Jeff Gray's was no exception. He had started working at Alton Grange the Easter before the rest of the probationers had arrived but for some reason no one had been out to see him from the Local Authority. Jeff's visit happened one Wednesday afternoon in late June. The weather had been good throughout the week and both Jeff and the children were sick of being cooped up in school. Jeff had 1C for science that afternoon. 1C were the least able class in the first year with a string of learning and behavioural problems. They were a real handful and Jeff knew that the last thing that they wanted to do on a warm summer's afternoon was to write about the life cycle of a frog. At lunchtime he mentioned to Arthur that he might be taking 1C for a walk to the local pond where they might see some frogs, and anyway it was such a nice day if they didn't learn anything then at least they were out in the sunshine. Arthur didn't bat an eye, he just told Jeff to be careful to bring as many back as he took out with him.

"Don't lose any of them or let them drown, there's too much paperwork to do if that happens", he said.

So the lesson came and Jeff's class could be heard going out of the building. Immediately it set off the inevitable, "can we go" around the classrooms. That central corridor with its glazed panels and the high walls to the exterior windows seemed to focus everything within school. Everyone knew what was going on in every classroom which wasn't always a bad thing especially if you needed help, but at times like this it was a bit of a nuisance. I imagine that it must be like that all the time in open plan classrooms and offices.

"How can we do geometry, while we're going for a walk?" I remember saying to 2A, who were struggling with congruency problems, and trying to quell the tide of 'can we go' questions.

Jeff can't have been gone for more than about ten minutes when Ned arrived, his characteristic hurried step clearly heard on the bare wooden floorboards of the corridor. As usual everything fell silent as we listened to hear what problem Ned was bringing for Arthur to solve. However, this time he wasn't alone. He was accompanied by a tall balding man in a light weight summer suit. The man looked very officious.

"Arthur", yelled Ned as usual, having just walked past Arthur's woodwork room.

Arthur came hurrying along the corridor.

"What's wrong Ned?" started Arthur, then seeing the other man, he added, "Oh, hello there, Paterson, deputy head" and he put out a sawdust coated hand to shake hands.

"Where's young Gray?" snapped Ned, "this' his inspector".

"Ah, yes," stumbled Arthur, "he's er, em, er, he's taken his class out".

"Out, out where?" snarled Ned.

"Oh, er, on a biological observation exercise", replied Arthur a worried look spreading across his face.

Ned's eyebrows raised. He was plainly impressed and thought that the inspector might also share that view.

"I'll send someone to tell him to come back into school, shall I?" said Arthur.

" Aye, right", said Ned in a much calmer voice, "we'll have a cuppa upstairs in the office, while he comes back".

Ned and the inspector clattered off down the corridor and up the stairs to the office. There was a quick knock on my classroom door and Arthur's head appeared.

"You'd hear all that," he said, "would you mind sending someone to bring Jeff's lot back into school?"

Arthur was talking to me, but a sea of hands went up volunteering to seek 1C on safari rather than struggle with the joys of congruency. Arthur looked around the class,

"Another popular lesson, I see."

He smiled and left me to sort it out.

"Edward, you're a good runner, aren't you?" I said, "go and tell Mr. Gray that an inspector's waiting to see him and that Mr. Walker wants him to come back straight away. Have you got that? Would you like a note?"

"Yes sir," said Edward, "I've got to find Mr. Gray and tell him that Ned, er, Mr. Walker says he's got to come back to school straight away to be inspected. But I don't think that he'll believe me".

" I'll write a note", I said to the boy.

I quickly wrote a note spelling out that it was a genuine inspection, gave it to Edward and off he went. I looked across the corridor and out through the open doors into the playground. In the distance I could see a cloud of dust moving along the edge of the colliery waste heap like the road runner of cartoon fame. I watched until I could see the dust travelling in the opposite direction then I knew that Edward was on his way back.

Just then Ned's voice could be heard booming down the corridor,

"Arthur, where the Hell's young Gray?"

The inspector frowned and shook his head. He had already made a judgement about Ned. Edward walked into the corridor just as Arthur was coming out of his room. Arthur said,

"He's been sent for, he'll be on his way back, they shouldn't be long, they've gone on some sort of biological survey".

"No, no, they haven't", interrupted Edward unable to contain himself, "Mr Gray took them for a walk up the pit heap to the pond 'cos it's a nice day instead of trying to teach them. And he says we can go next time. That's what he said when I give him the note".

The three men looked at each other. Nothing was said but they all knew what each other was thinking.

My own probationary inspection took place the following week, again with no prior warning and from my point of view it couldn't have happened at a worse time. Unusually I had been told to cover a lesson at the upper school. This was unusual in as much as the majority of staff basically worked on one of the sites and only rarely taught on the other site. Cover for absent colleagues was generally available from 'free' staff on each site and it was not often that someone had to move site to cover a lesson. However, on this occasion I was unlucky enough to be the only person 'free' and there were several staff absent at the upper school. I was to cover a lesson for Bill Blackburn who was out on a training course. I had no idea what class or what subject I would be covering. I arrived at the upper school to find that it was 3C for practical maths. This was another of Ned's inventions for filling the timetable when conventional lessons didn't fit. It was a mixture of geometry, technical drawing and art with a lot of compass work, measuring angles, drawing triangles and colouring in. There was no scheme of work or book to follow and no sequence of lessons: you just "made it up as you went along", I was told. I have to say that most staff who knew that they were going to have to occupy children with these lessons had actually sat down and prepared a 'course' of some type. Some staff had tried to make it a bit more light hearted by drawing and colouring in flowers, patterns and buildings, but Bill wasn't like most people. As a very strict, almost perfectionist technical drawing teacher, he saw this extra lesson as an opportunity for some serious additional drawing. The problem was that 3C were the least able class in year three and possibly the least dextrous group of children known to mankind! They were also a very difficult group to manage with a myriad of learning difficulties and behavioural problems.

As soon as they saw me coming along the corridor they moaned, which surprised me as I had really had very little to do with them in the past. I ignored it and went into the room having already decided to be a complete contrast to Bill in terms of my approach – big mistake; at that stage in my teaching experience I had not realised that most children respond to the room, their expectations of what will go on in it, what part they will play in that lesson and how they are usually managed, to a much greater extent than who is actually stood in front of them and I was proposing to change all of that.

I had inwardly panicked when I was told who I would be taking but I had followed the advice of another teacher,

"Don't worry, Bill will have left something for them to do and if he hasn't, remember, the best lesson plan is a long walk from the staffroom".

It had been along walk from the staffroom to Bill's classroom, a very long walk and I had planned to help the children to draw a simple flower with pencil and compass then colour it in, at least as a start to the lesson.

However, it wasn't to be when I looked at the instructions carefully sellotaped to the teacher's desk. Bill had all of the work mapped out; written up in minute detail with times allocated to each step and additional work for those children who had finished before the rest and so on. It was so well presented that I felt obliged to try to stick with it and do as Bill wanted.

They were to construct some equilateral triangles, each containing an inscribed circle, given the appropriate dimensions and using only pencils, compasses and rulers.

I explained the task to a chorus of moans and groans culminating in "I can't do that" "we done that last week" and "this is boring". Arthur Johnson happened to be passing, heard the noise and knocked on the door, then pushed his head into the room. The class immediately fell silent.

"Ah, 3C", said Arthur, "voices like angels".

Arthur caught sight of Johnny Bates out of the corner of his eye. Johnny was gazing out of the window paying no attention at all. Arthur looked across the room at Johnny raised his voice slightly and said,

"Every good boy deserves?"

" Flogging", replied Johnny instinctively.

"Excellent", replied Arthur, "don't forget it.... Flogging".

With that he closed the door and was gone. He had said nothing directly to me and I'm sure that his intention had been to settle the class and let them know that he was on the prowl. It was meant to be supportive but it actually made things worse and had really unsettled the class who until that point had not been too bad.

I tried to settle the class down and make a start on the work. I was just feeling that things were getting out of control and the children were a bit boisterous when Ned appeared at the end of the corridor.

The upper school classrooms all had glass panels in one side facing onto a stone floored corridor. This gave a good view of the corridor and you could here anyone moving about in it. We could hear the clatter of Ned's shoes on the corridor floor. Ned had a stranger with him. Ned flung open the classroom door.

"This is Mr. Clarke, chief inspector for the County. He's here to see you teach", balled Ned.

"Thank you, Mr. Walker. Er, come in. Have a seat", I stumbled to say, obviously anxious and a complete bundle of nerves.

By now the class were very restless and had also heard Ned's announcement. The more astute among them realised that this was an opportunity for their favourite pastime: 'teacher baiting', and if they started the rest would follow their lead.

I tried to settle them down and get them back on task thinking that if they were busy they might be more manageable. But in those few minutes of introductions something had already started. Two boys towards the back of the class were on their feet pushing each other about and issuing all sorts of threats to each other. I hurried to the back of the room, told them both to sit down at opposite sides of the room and get on with their work. To my amazement they did just that and the rest of the class seemed to settle.

For a few minutes everything seemed to be going well. The inspector had started wandering about the room looking at the immaculate drawings on the wall and the work in the children's books. He stopped and asked one or two if they liked practical maths and how was it different from technical drawing. The children were just about to answer when a dart flew across the room sticking into the cheek of Trevor Jones with the sort of thud that it might have made going into a dartboard. There was actually very little blood but the drama that erupted was horrendous. Trevor was obviously shocked, as were the rest of the children and I suspect the inspector. Children were shouting at each other. Trevor was screaming with the pain of the dart and holding on to it trying to stop it from bleeding. Chaos had broken out in a matter of seconds.

My first concern was for Trevor. I rushed across the room to his assistance telling him not to pull the dart out and I would get some help. Suddenly the classroom door was thrown open and Arthur Johnson walked in.

"Quiet!" he said calmly but firmly.

The noise stopped immediately.

"Perhaps, you'd like to take young Jones out, Mr. Walters", said Arthur, "while I deal with whoever's responsible for this disruption to your lesson. I think I need to talk to 3C".

I helped Trevor from his seat and out into the corridor. He was crying and obviously in pain.

"We'll go down to the office, and get someone to deal with this", I said trying to comfort the boy.

The inspector came out of the room with me.

"Not very good, was it?" he said, "I'll come back another day."

He headed off towards Ned's office.

That was it. I thought that my very short teaching career had just ended. However, Trevor was still my immediate concern. By this time Madeline Watson, the domestic science teacher had come out of her classroom which was just opposite. She was carrying a tea towel, which she wrapped around Trevor's face, the dart still in place.

"Stop that snivelling," she said to the boy, "this tea towel's clean. It'll stop the bleeding but heaven knows how I'll get it clean by the time you've finished."

She looked at me and said,

"I'll see to him. You'd best go back to your class."

I went back to the class feeling very despondent and worried about the events of the last few minutes. I could see through the corridor windows that the class were all busy working in silence as Arthur prowled among them, making comments on the quality of their work.

"This is the culprit. I hope that you don't mind, but I've dealt with it," he announced as I walked through the classroom door.

He pulled Tony Evans from his seat by his right ear. The boy was obviously in pain but said nothing.

"We've had a bit of a chat about it; seems it's an on going feud. But it's about to stop. And the rest of them know that their behaviour was not acceptable when a visitor was in school. They've let themselves and the school down," said Arthur, the volume of his voice increasing as he got to the end of the sentence and the tone markedly changed.

"Thanks for your help, Mr. Johnson," I said.

"You don't need my help, lad," said Arthur, "we're all in this together. We work as a team. We work together. One problem is everybody's problem".

I didn't know how to respond and was probably still in shock. Much later, I realised that Arthur's comments were aimed at the class more than me, but what he had said was certainly true and made a lasting impression on me which I used throughout the rest of my career.

Arthur left the room and thankfully the bell rang for break. I quickly got the class to clear up and dismissed them thinking that it was best to make no more of the incident and that Tony had already been punished. I rushed down to Madeline Watson's room to find out what had happened to Trevor, expecting to find at least an ambulance, irate parents and the police. To my relief and surprise I found Trevor sitting in an armchair in the 'home area' of the domestic science room, with no sign of the dart just a small elastoplast on his face. He was smiling as he ate one of Madeline's famous warm scones, the butter and jam dripping from the corner of his mouth.

"He's as right as rain," said Madeline, "these things often look much worse than they are. We just took the dart out, cleaned him up a bit and there you are. Would you like a scone?"

I had had very little to do with Madeline until that day but she'd sorted everything out, while she had her own class, and given me enormous support. I was very grateful. My words must have seemed totally inadequate,

"Thanks, thanks very much for all your help. I won't have a scone. I'd better get back to the bottom school."

And with that I left Trevor eating his scone quite unperturbed by what had happened. I rushed back to the lower school just in time for the next lesson to begin and no time to speak to anyone.

Just before the end of the day, Arthur popped his head around the classroom door and said,

"I could do with a few words before you go. OK?"

"Yes. That's fine," I said. But I was actually thinking: this is it, he's going to tell me that I'm finished.

The bell rang for the end of the lesson and I dismissed the class. Within a few minutes Arthur came into the room.

"I've had Ned on the phone," he said, "seems like things didn't go too well when the inspector was in".

"No," I said, " it was a shambles and that business with the dart. I just couldn't believe it".

"Look, lad," said Arthur, "don't worry, we all have difficult lessons when things don't go as they should, and the dart problem was a one off. You can't be held responsible for a lunatic throwing darts about the room. You dealt with it. The inspector will come back and you won't be on a cover lesson with a class that you shouldn't be teaching. It'll be fine. You've made a good start here. You can do this job and do it well. Believe me I would have told you if you were no good at it. You get on with everyone, everyone staff and kids. They like you. Don't be put off by one bad lesson like this, one lesson that you shouldn't have been taking when an inspector was coming in. So don't dwell on it. Go home and forget about it. We'll see you tomorrow."

With that Arthur left. I felt a bit more reassured but still very shaken. I felt unable to talk about it and knew that it would be the talk of the school for days to come.

The next few days were a bit of a nightmare. Every little problem seemed to be enormous. Every time that there was a noise in the corridor I imagined that it was Ned with the Inspector but nothing happened until the following week.

It was Thursday afternoon and I had just started an English lesson with 1A when I heard footsteps in the corridor and saw Arthur and another man coming towards me. Arthur knocked on the door and came in,

"Mr. Clarke to see you, Mr. Walters."

There was no mention to the children that the man was an inspector. Arthur smiled and gestured to Mr. Clarke to go to the back of the room. I recognised Mr. Clarke immediately and smiled that forced smile that we all do in these situations and I thought that I'd do my best, as I always did to make the lesson interesting and enjoyable. The lesson was at that stage where we were reading around the class. The book was once again "White Fang"(there were very few sets of class readers in the school). I was asking pupils to read a paragraph to the rest of the class, then I would ask questions to ensure that we all understood the story, or particular vocabulary, or the style in which the book was written. I had built up a good relationship with 1A and I suspect that they realised that the lesson was important to me. Perhaps they had guessed who the man was but unusually and thankfully no one asked.

The lesson passed without incident. Lots of children were happy to read, some were a little more reluctant but no one refused. They all seemed to understand the short written task towards the end of the lesson and almost everyone appeared to be interested and on task as the inspector talked to some of them. I had to speak to one or two girls about their attention wandering but it was late in the day.

The lesson came to an end and the class left. The inspector walked towards me.

"Don't look so worried," he said, my face showing my anxiety, "it was good. They liked you. They liked the story and almost all were trying to get something from it without being pinned to the wall with darts."

He started to laugh.

" So," he went on," that's it. I've seen a good lesson. I've talked to Mr. Paterson who thinks you're going to be an excellent teacher, so I'm pleased to tell you that you have satisfied the requirements of your probationary year and you are now a fully qualified teacher. Well done."

He held out his hand. We shook hands and I said,

"Thanks very much."

"And don't worry. Anyone can have a poor lesson especially when you've got some unhinged clown in the class. I'll just have a word with Mr. Paterson before I go."

I was amazed. That was it. It was over. I'd passed. The relief was incredible.

Since that day I've seen more inspectors than I care to remember and none of them have left me feeling so relieved as that inspection with Mr. Clark.

Once again I was in Arthur's debt and very grateful for his support. He had handled the whole business in a totally different way to Ned and although he would never criticise Ned for allowing the inspector to see me during a cover lesson, I felt sure that it would not have happened if I had been at the lower school with Arthur in charge. I have used his words with other teachers many times since that chat after the first dramatic inspector's visit.

14

SPORTS DAY

The end of term and particularly the end of the summer term can be a very difficult time in school. Staff and children are tired, looking forward to the holidays not least as a break away from each other and perhaps a time for something a little different. It may well be a time dreaded by many parents but it was always a blessed relief to me and I'm sure many other teachers as well.

Of course it was also a part of the school year when there might be trips out, visits and events that made the trials of the last few weeks a little less tedious for the children but often made life much more stressful for the teachers with the added burden of reports, recommendations for class changes and finishing things off.

At Alton Grange anything that cost the school or parents money was out of the question. The school was being run on a shoe string and many of the parents had little or no money to spare, but home spun events were encouraged. Probably the most important of these was Sports Day. A day in the school calendar when the school could 'show off its sporting prowess' and more significantly from the children's perspective, a day with no taught lessons. Everyone was expected to take part in some way: everyone except Ned who was "going to a very important meeting at County Hall, whenever it was."

The P.E. staff saw Sports Day as their big day and to be fair most of the children seemed to be looking forward to it, and not just to avoid lessons. The build up lasted for about a fortnight and involved having a running track white lined onto one of the playing fields at the top school site and collecting together the props that would be needed for the events. Local schools staggered their sports days so that they could share whatever resources they had.

George Raine and I were given responsibility for the public announcements and commentary. This was common practice in most schools where the science staff were expected to be experts with the public address system or anything else vaguely technical. Although I had taught general subjects all year, this was the one occasion when I suddenly became part of the science staff. Jeff Gray also worked in science but was a keen sportsman and had been commandeered by the P.E. department to organise the relay events. George had it all under control having done it many times before and he loved this sort of thing anyway. I was happy to remain in the background as the 'technical help'.

Knowing that the weather could easily be poor and it would probably rain, as it generally does on school sports days, George had decided to borrow a tent from the boy scouts so that at least the electrical equipment could be kept under cover. The tent was organised to arrive a few days before the event, shortly after the scouts had used it on one of their jamborees.

As well as the official teams and events organised by the P.E. department, form teachers were expected to organise teams for the less athletic events, the fun events like the sack race, potato and spoon race (it used to be egg and spoon but it was too messy, all those broken eggs) and the famous wellie hoying event. Organising form teams turned out to be a real performance, with more arguments about who was good at this, or who would or wouldn't take part. In my form group one example involved a boy called Danny Evans. He was considered to be a good runner by the other children in the class but when he was asked to take part he said that he didn't know whether he'd be able to run.

"What's the problem, Danny?" I asked.

"Well sir, it depends on if I'm up in time," answered Danny.

"What d'yer mean? Up in time?" I asked.

"Yer know, if I get the right clothes or if our Billy gets the best and there's nowt left fer me."

I was puzzled by the conversation but I thought that I'd better not pursue it in case there was a problem with clothing in the household. That morning break the problem was solved quite by accident.

Margaret and Jeff were having a conversation about the way that some of the children were dressed. I mentioned what Danny had said.

"Well, that's probably right," said Jeff.

I must have looked puzzled, still not understanding what he meant because he went on, "in some of these families they all sleep in the same room to keep warm, especially in the winter. When they go to bed they just throw their clothes into a pile on the floor. Whoever gets up first, gets first choice from the pile on the floor. So last up gets what's left."

"Oh, I see. That explains why Danny was coming to school last week in a pink jumper that I'm sure I had seen his sister wearing the week before," I said realising what had happened.

Then the real seriousness of the situation began to dawn. The Evans' were one of the many squatter families that we had in school. They had had a hard time since the pit had closed and they had been evicted from their colliery house. There was no work, very little money and no permanent home. Life was pretty grim for these families.

"I'm sure that we can find some P.E. kit, some shorts and a top at least," I began to say, but was interrupted by Margaret.

"The trouble is," she said, "I hope you don't mind me putting my two pennyworth in but you're got to be very careful not to hurt their pride, not to show any favouritism and not to start something that they'll all want."

Of course this was very sensible advice, especially as I knew that Margaret often brought clothes into school for children that her own children had grown out of.

"Leave it with me," said Margaret, "Danny shall go to the ball..,er, sports day, even if he needs a little help from me."

I knew that Margaret would be as good as her word, so I left it at that point.

Sports day finally arrived. Registration was very noisy, all of the children very excited at the prospect of the day. Danny was proudly wearing white shorts, black plimsolls and a rugby shirt that looked amazingly like that of another Durham school.

"Like me shirt?" said Danny, "Mrs. Jackson thought that I might like it better than me jumper."

" Well, you really look the part," I said, "now all you've got to do is win."

" No bother, that's the easy bit," smiled Danny delighted with his 'new' kit.

The day had been organised in two parts with field events in the morning and athletics and fun events in the afternoon when parents could come to spectate if they wished. The children from the bottom school were going to commute together to the top school after morning registration. We were to meet in the main hall then form a crocodile along the Front Street and gradually make our way through the council estate to the playing fields at the top school.

The children were waiting quietly in the hall for the message to tell them to start the journey when Ned's footsteps could be heard coming down the corridor. Ned rarely came into assemblies or any large gathering of children, so this was most unusual. As he walked to the front of the hall looking for Arthur, he spotted a second year boy who seemed to be giving off a bright beam of light. Arthur had just arrived and was about to tell the children to start making their way to the top school. Ned was looking around wondering what was causing the light when he noticed that it was the sun reflecting from an earring in the boy's left ear.

"What the bloody Hell's that?" boomed Ned, "get it out, at once! We're not havin' any puffs or pirates in my school! Arthur its time you got this lot sorted out. The place is going to be full o' nancy boys afore we kna where we at. I'm off t' County Hall. I'll see yer, tomorrow."

He turned and stormed out of the hall and up the corridor glaring at the children as he went. Arthur said nothing but the expression on his face reflected what everyone was thinking.

We set off for the top school passing Ned's car outside the butchers. You could tell immediately that it was Ned's car because it looked like a mobile ash tray and still had that nasty stain down the dashboard where he spilt a bottle of milk months before and not cleaned it up properly. As we passed the shop Ned came bustling out, a white paper parcel under his arm,

"Come on, out the way," he boomed, "I'm supposed to be at County Hall by now."

The children, and everyone else for that matter, moved out of the way stepping onto the road to let him past. Ned charged through, narrowly missing an elderly lady with a walking stick. In his haste to reach the car he stepped in some fresh horse manure that had just been left by the horse pulling Mr. Thubron's log and stick cart along the Main Street.

"Oh, bugger it," he said as he climbed into the car and sped off.

When we arrived at the top school I had arranged to send my form group to the P.E. staff while I went to find George and the public address system. I soon spotted them as I turned the corner of the main building and walked out onto the playing field. The tent was still being erected, it hadn't been delivered as arranged. It was an enormous white bell tent looking like something from Billy Smart's circus. As I walked a little closer the full spectacle was even more absurd. The tent was old and dirty with curious brown stains along one side and it had a peculiar smell.

George was dressed in khaki shorts and matching short sleeved shirt. He only needed the white pith helmet to have been at home in "the Bridge over the River Kwai" or perhaps "It Ain't Half Hot

Mum" would have been more appropriate. He was standing behind a table covered in metal boxes with lots of wires coming out of them leading to an enormous trumpet like loud speaker. As I walked into the tent he saw me and

"One, two, one, two, " crackled from the loud speaker as George adjusted the controls.

"We've been given another job for this afternoon," said George.

"Oh, have we?" I replied.

"What's that then?" I said as I looked around the inside of the tent and really started to notice the smell. It was a mixture of damp and ammonia.

"What on Earth have they being using this thing for?" I said turning my attention back to George.

He was pointing a gun at me trying to look menacing but he couldn't help laughing at the startled expression that must have been on my face.

"We've got to start the races, only this thing's not working properly. The plan is to show it to the competitors, then count down from three and shout "bang!" at the appropriate time," he said.

"That sounds convincing," I replied sarcastically.

"I'll see if I can get it working before this afternoon," said George, "I expect that's really why they've given it to us."

I wasn't keen on the 'us'. I was looking forward to a quiet day in the background not a star part in the limelight.

"If I do the starting," George went on, "you'll have to do the commentary on the races."

" I've never done anything like that before," I said anxiously.

"Oh, you just make it up as you go along," said George, "you just talk about which race it is, who's taking part, yer know, that sort of thing. You'll be fine."

I'll be fine wasn't what I was thinking. No quiet day in the background then.

The morning passed with few incidents as the children took part in the field events. The highlight was Terry Booth, the R.E. teacher, dressed as a Zulu warrior in full make up and costume directing the javelin throwing. My job was to relay messages and pass on notices to competitors giving me some opportunity to familiarise myself with the microphone and operating the amplifier. The afternoon was to be the main event starting at two o'clock in the hope that some parents might attend.

"Do you usually find that many parents come?" I said to George.

"Oh, yes," replied George, "it's taken over from the old field days and picnics that they used to have when the pit was working. There'll be a few stalls and a coconut shy provided by the W.I, the Boys' Brigade and such like and of course Albert will send someone up to sell ice cream."

There was a pause as George looked at the starting pistol not really taking much notice of my questions. Then he went on,

"I can't get this pistol to work. I don't know whether it's jammed or dirty: whatever it is it won't fire. George pointed the pistol in the air and pulled the trigger. "Bang" went the gun.

All of the people near to the tent jumped, then came running to see what was happening. George was delighted,

"Oh, great. Now we'll be able to do it properly. Look, announce the call for the first race and we'll make a start."

George ran off to the start line, waving the gun as he went.

"First year boys, 100 metre sprint to the start line, please," I heard myself saying into the microphone.

So it had started and before I had realised what was happening I was calling for other competitors, reading out the results and passing on information feeling a lot more confident than I had been earlier in the day. Everything seemed to be going well until a girl arrived with a message from Simon Bateson, Head of P.E. telling me to give the audience more of a commentary on the races rather than just announcements and results. I really had no idea what to do because I hadn't attended any athletic meetings as such and my own school sports days were best forgotten and didn't have a commentary anyway. I wondered what might be suitable. I'd seen horse racing on the television and thought that style might be just the thing to liven things up.

The next race was the second year boys 1500 metres relay and I recognised more of the children taking part because I taught most of them so I thought I'd put the idea to the test.

George fired the pistol and the boys started to run. I immediately started on the commentary,

"And they're off, with Billy Neilson on the nearside followed by John Gilday and Edward Mortimer. And whose this bringing up the rear, it's Charlie Childs in the wellies."

Charlie was actually running in mid July in black wellingtons turned down at the ankle to shorten them: probably all that he had to wear and no one was in the least concerned.

"And as they come into the final furlong, it's Billy by a short head. And, yes as they pass the post it's Billy. Billy first followed by Edward and John. I'm sure you'll agree a remarkable display. But, just a minute. Who's this limping up the outside lane. Yes, it's Charlie. Let's hear it for Charlie."

The crowd clapped and cheered as Charlie staggered over the finishing line, a broad smile on his face.

I managed to keep going in a similar style for the next few races until Arthur Johnson came hurrying over to the tent, looking very annoyed.

"It's meant to be a school sports day," he snapped glaring at me, "not a day at the races."

He stormed off clearly not amused. To be honest it was very much like 'a day at the races' …. of Marx Brother's fame.

By now the starting pistol had stopped working again and George was trying to manage by showing the competitors the gun, counting them down from three to one then shouting 'bang!' I continued to make the announcements, give the score and call for missing competitors while moderating my commentary.

We were nearing the end of the day when John Young ambled into the tent looking pretty miserable.

"What's wrong John?" I asked.

"Mr. Johnson says I'm stupid, that I've let his class down," blurted out John. "I didn't see the gun or hear the bang and when I looked up, they'd all gone. Then I tripped over my shoelace and I think I've broken my glasses," he continued.

He removed his glasses, which had only one arm and the bridge was held in place by a dirty sticky plaster, and passed them towards me. Without actually taking them from him I said,

"They look to be in a bad way already, I think you'll need some new ones."

John snatched them back.

"Can't have any. Me mam says they're too dear and I wouldn't like them anyway."

"How long have you had them?" I asked.

"Since the juniors," replied John.

"I really think that you could do with some new ones," I said, "perhaps I can find out how you go about it, then let you know."

"Right, OK then," said John and off he went seemingly much happier, but in fact he'd just noticed one of Alberto Valdersera's son's on a 'stop me and buy one' tricycle and was dashing off for an ice cream.

I muddled through the afternoon until it finally came to the last event of the day. A girl arrived at the tent doorway with a note from Simon Bateson. The message said 'please tell all competitors for the wellie hoying to collect in the middle of the field'. So that's what I read out. There was a stampede of excited children rushing towards the centre of the field, followed almost at once by a hail of wellingtons that seemed to be going in all directions, including some hurling towards Madeline Watson's cake stall.

"If any of those wellies come over here," she snapped, "and anything is gets damaged, there'll be Hell on! Chapman, where's Brian Chapman? This'll be another one of his daft ideas."

The afternoon came to a close with the presentation of awards to individual competitors, winning teams and winning form groups. Arthur Paterson made the presentations after making excuses for Ned. George took control of the equipment, much to my relief, and there was a return to a more conventional commentary that it seems was expected. However, I was surprised by the comments made by some parents who seemed to have appreciated my 'new' style. I had learned a valuable lesson about expectation: the need to conform, what ever the standards. Of course it would have been helpful to have been told what was expected in the first place.

Soon after sports day the term came to an end: it seemed to just stop. There was no wind down or other activities to mark the occasion. Everyone was expecting news of a merger with the other secondary schools in the area but nothing happened; apparently a merger had been expected for the previous fifteen years – perhaps that explained the disgraceful condition of the bottom school buildings.

I had survived that initial year of teaching. I had witnessed the impact of the destruction of the Durham coalfield. I had managed to fulfil the probationary requirements and learned an enormous amount about people, managing children and what really goes on in schools. All of these things were to stand me in good stead for the coming years which was just as well because as Arthur said,

"You've had a good year and in another ten or so you'll make a good teacher."

As always he was right, but now it was time to get on with my own life.

APPENDIX

THE MEANING OF SOME PITMATIC WORDS.

The meaning of some of the less obvious pitmatic words used by some of the characters, particularly Ned.

Pitmatic – a dialect of Durham's mining community

Aye – yes

Bairns – children
Blaa – blow
Blether – to talk nonsense
Byeuts – boots

Card – cold
Claes – clothes
Clag – stick
Clarty – dirty
Cree – a garden shed

Dee – do

Fettle – good condition

Gan – go

Hadaway – go away
Hoy – throw
Hyem – home

Ket – sweets

Knaa – know

Mair – more

Nee – no
Nyem – name

Oot – out

Pet – a term of endearment

Sandshoes – gym shoes
Snaa – snow

Tab – cigarette
Tatie – potato
Telt – told
Thowt – thought
Tret – treated

Us – me

Wey – Why
Whe – Who

Yersel – yourself
Ye,yer – you, your

www.ingramcontent.com/pod-product-compliance
Ingram Content Group UK Ltd.
Pitfield, Milton Keynes, MK11 3LW, UK
UKHW020133250726
13967UKWH00002B/623

9 781425 180133